MOUTH SEWN SHUT

By

GREG SLAP

FIRST STITCH

THE CELL PHONE RANG AND VIBRATED on the table next to me. As grating as the sound was, I did my best to ignore it, allowing the small plastic device to jiggle its way toward the edge of the table where it was bound to drop to the floor.

Fresh ideas were hard to come by, so when the concept for an illustration finally hit, I began working feverishly to get it on paper. The idea for the drawing, a pen-and-ink of a lake, had come to me inexplicably, as if by some divine design. In a moment of fanatical inspiration, I began drawing a surreal lake with the San Gabriel Mountains in the distance. Oddly, I'd never seen anything like it. I'd never seen a lake surrounded by scraggly trees, black river rocks, or wild grasses like these. Even so, the concept worked. It had a mysterious feel while still merging organic elements, all features the client had asked for. It felt good to be on a roll like this; when artistic rolls came, there was no sense in stopping to wonder what had brought them on or worrying too much if my fucking phone rang.

As the phone buzzed its way to the edge of the drafting table, I hurried to fill in rocks one at a time. Whoever was calling could wait, I told myself, but when I glanced briefly at the face of the cell and saw it was my buddy Trey, I picked it up.

"Hey, what're you doing?" Trey asked, sounding slow and sleepy.

"Working on that proposal. You know, the new client I told you about."

"Yeah...Yeah, I remember now. A magazine...or was it a book deal?"

"Both, I hope. What's up?" I asked, sensing something was bothering him.

He was high, not sleepy like I'd thought before. When Trey was high, he spoke slower and his voice got deeper, which were two ways of telling.

"You know when old shit starts popping up, like out of nowhere? Like I was thinking about my mom just now. It's fuckin' weird, 'cause I don't talk to her much. Then I started thinking about how she has a way of putting her shit on me. Dude, it's like, somehow she hurts more than anyone else. Somehow she knows what's best, even when she's fucking up."

The other way I could tell Trey was high was that he got into his personal shit, something he didn't do unless he was stoned or drunk. He may've been stoned and talking weird, but there was no hiding that he was also tense and pissed. So I listened. With my phone cocked between my cheek and shoulder, while working on darkening the massive lake in my drawing—dot by dot—I let him talk, figuring he needed to unload, get stuff out.

While he talked, I filled in rocks with the needle-fine point of my pen. It was late, and the only light came from a small desk lamp on my drafting table. A table I'd set up in the dining room area of my one-bedroom apartment. The area most people used for eating or entertaining, I used for my freelance illustration work. It was no more than an extension of the living room, and since it overlooked the quiet residential street outside, it offered a sense of being outdoors. During the day, when I did most of my work, there was the added advantage of natural light.

Trey began telling me about his welfare, food-stamp upbringing and how he resented his mom for it. I'd not known any of this about him. In fact, I knew little about his childhood. Up until now our personal talks had been limited to chicks, relationships with coworkers, girlfriends, our goals and plans for our respective artistic careers, but rarely about shit like this.

He said that, although he'd resented his mom for her neglectful upbringing, he hadn't hated her until the day he'd walked in on her and his former best friend.

"Imagine that..." Trey stopped before going on. "Walking in on your own fucking mom blowing the dude you'd been friends with since middle school... That sucks, bro."

"Fuck, that's sick. How old were you?" I asked, feeling weird about digging too much.

"I was a senior in high school, so I figure I was about seventeen."

Then it happened. Stuff like it has happened to me before, like in lucid dreams and shit, but never like this, not this real. First a sudden feeling of nausea came over me, and I set my pen down so I wouldn't ruin the drawing with an ink spill. Then, as the nausea got worse, I tried swallowing to keep myself from vomiting, but it got so bad I had to close my eyes to stop the dizziness.

When I opened my eyes again, the dizziness had passed, but I wasn't in my studio anymore. I was in a dimly lit, bohemian-like, overly furnished bedroom. The smell of recently smoked weed and incense came at me from the side of a big messed-up bed. Sitting on the edge was a woman who was busy sucking off this skinny black kid who stood in front of her. His eyes were closed, and he balanced himself with a hand that gripped the woman's shoulder.

There was no sound. The only thing I could hear was my own heavy breathing, until I heard Trey's voice over the phone say, "Fuck that shit..." just like I would've if I'd been back in my apartment.

The kid in the vision was talking, or maybe moaning, because even though his mouth moved, his eyes remained closed. Then the woman pulled her mouth away, releasing his cock so she could laugh before resuming her work; I saw these things, but I didn't hear them. So when the door next to the bed suddenly flew open and I saw a much younger Trey standing in the doorway, I froze with shock and slipped into a helpless fascination.

"I went in her room like I always did after school, and fucking Jerome was there...with my mom blowing him," I heard Trey say sadly, somewhere over the phone, a phone I no longer felt on my cheek—not here in this room, anyway.

By now, I sensed that moving and speaking were not options for me. Although I stood still to avoid being detected, it didn't seem necessary; it became more and more evident that Trey and the other people in the vision were unable to see me. Because I couldn't move, all I could do was stare at Trey—the high school Trey—the woman, and the kid standing at her feet. It was a lot like coming alive in a silent movie, like being the sole observer while the actors went about their business.

The expression on the younger Trey's face was a sad combination of shock, anger, and disbelief. He stood frozen in place, his backpack hanging near his feet, his mouth open, as if all he could do was stare. Then his expression changed into something hard, and he clenched his jaw like he was getting ready to fight.

But Trey didn't fight. He lifted his backpack with both hands and tossed it at his friend's head, just like he was passing a basketball. Then he turned and walked away.

"All I could do was fucking toss my books at him," Trey said loudly over the phone, managing to wake me out of my vision or whatever it had been. I was back at my desk, turning in my seat, looking around my apartment frantically, taking in my things just to be sure this was real. *What the fuck just happened? Why did it feel so real?*

Although I was back home, whatever had happened to me was disorienting. Hell, one second I'd been in a strange woman's bedroom seeing my friend as a teenager, and now I was back.

Still in my chair, I settled, took a few deep breaths, tightened my hold on the cell to avoid dropping it, and tried listening to Trey. It took what seemed like minutes for me to chill, but I couldn't talk just yet. The shock of seeing—no, it was more the shock of actually *being in* another place totally freaked me out.

After a few more deep and slow breaths, my heart slowed its pounding, and I started to feel better. I almost told Trey about what I'd just "seen." Since his story matched the picture in my head so well, I wanted to tell him, but I didn't—which later, much later, would prove advantageous.

Besides, there were some differences between what I'd seen and Trey's story. He said he'd thrown his books, but I'd seen him toss a big backpack at the kid. Also, he'd not described his mom's room, which meant all those details—the red handkerchief over the bedside lamp, the incense, all of those things—were things I must have imagined.

Trey kept on talking, and I listened, waiting for a pause. A big part of me was eager to say something, not only to test out my voice but to be sure this conversation was real. "Man, Trey." This was all I could come up with. "I hope you beat the crap out of the dickhead, even if he was your friend."

"I did, sort of. I hit him pretty hard; all my books were in my backpack. The thing I feel bad about was how fuckin' hard I let my mom have it. Dude, I said some bad shit to her later…to my own mother."

Okay, big deal. I'd imagined a backpack and I was right. No David Blaine shit here. Besides, the coincidence stopped there, because in my "vision" the woman I'd seen as Trey's mom was white, fat, and had tons of curly blonde hair, and Trey was black. *Why would I imagine a white woman as the mother of my black friend?* I asked myself, not sure if there was an answer. *Maybe my visions were as ethnocentric as I was.*

To be honest, the more I mentally rationalized with myself, the more convinced I was that it wasn't such a big surprise I'd imagined any of it. My imagination tends to be much more active than most people's. Shit, my whole life and livelihood depended on my ability to envision things.

Just a week before, I'd had a discussion with a friend about the visual acuity of artists. When people tell us shit, our minds race involuntarily with all kinds of pictures. It was the clearness of the strange bedroom and the sense of being there that unnerved me. *Fuck, I'd even smelled her weed.*

"Hey, whatever you said to her, it seems she had it coming, you know? That's disturbing shit, seeing her with a buddy like that." This wasn't me bullshitting him, I truly believe he had every right to mouth off to his mom.

I really wanted him to go on, to tell me more, but I didn't want to force him into it. Then I heard Trey take a long deep breath, and I worried he might be crying. It wasn't until I heard him exhale slowly that I realized he'd been taking a pretty deep hit from his joint.

As soon as I felt calmer, I carefully picked up my rapidograph pen and began to stipple the water's edge while waiting for Trey to talk, glad when he finally did.

"Duffy was full-on white trash," Trey said. "All the way from abusing food stamps to selling dope to my buddies for extra cash. Let's just say my mom would've been right at home in a trailer."

This caught me off guard. Was Duffy his mom? "Who's Duffy?"

"My mom," Trey said.

"Dude, your mom's white? Your real mom...is white?" I was shocked. Mostly it was hard to believe that Trey, who I'd thought was all black, had a white mom. The accuracy of my vision, the hallucination I'd just had, hadn't registered—*yet.*

"Yeah, I'm dark like my dad, but Duffy's white, all right. Anyway, I don't really like talking about her much. Maybe I'm a little ashamed of her."

Fine. I'd seen a white woman blowing that kid. Not entirely unimaginable. Maybe Trey had mentioned her and I'd forgotten, so I didn't go into it. It was just a weird vision that ended up being more coincidence than anything psychic on my part.

"Hey, man, listen. I've got to get this proposal done before the end of the week, and—"

"No worries. I'm wiped out, I think I can finally get some sleep. Hey, thanks for, ah...thanks for listening."

"No problem...Hey, I guess I'll see you at Craig's." A friend from the Art Center was having a party, and we'd both been invited.

"I'll be there. And I'll be by tomorrow, before heading over to Melrose," Trey reminded me.

Before heading to bed, I stood back and took in my work. It was a good first draft. It wasn't finished; there were rocks, shadows, skyline, and grasses that still needed to be added, but it was a strong piece. It was a great start.

The next morning, after breakfast and a half hour of radio news, I went right back to working on the drawing. It was tedious and repetitive work, especially filling in those rocks—there must've been thousands of them—but if I let my mind wander, it became therapeutic in an odd way. The vision I'd had while on the phone with Trey had made its way to the back of my mind. It hid, but it wouldn't be gone for long.

At about eleven, I heard a knock on my door and knew it was Trey. I didn't want to get up just yet, so I called out, "Come in."

The door opened and Trey stomped in. "Hey. You're really into that drawing." He stood behind me and glanced over my shoulder to get a look. "Nice... very nice. Dude, you have a knack for tiny details. Those trees, that mass of—"

"It'll be water, a small lake," I interrupted, mostly to clarify.

"Cool," he called over his shoulder as he went to the kitchen.

"Yeah, it's a good client. If they go with this concept, it'll be pretty good money."

When I raised my head to look, he was opening cabinets in search of a mug. Seconds later, I heard him pour a cup of coffee, fumble with the microwave door, and press some buttons that beeped loudly before he slammed the microwave door shut.

"Fuck, Trey, go easy on the microwave, dude."

After stretching my back, I got up and joined him in the kitchen. Trey had the fridge open and was popping the cap off the milk. He brought it up to his nose, then held it out to me and asked, "This fresh?"

There was no need to answer him. Trey had a tendency to ask questions he would go about answering on his own, so I wasn't surprised when he took a swig and ended up pouring the milk into his now heated coffee.

"I'm making the gallery rounds." Trey meant he was shopping his portfolio to local galleries. Since I lived just off Melrose, where tons of the hottest galleries were located, he often came to hang out before stomping the pavement and showing his work to potential locales.

Trey's work was awesome; his last series, which featured surreal and muted paintings of birds with human characteristics, had sold well. But the gallery he'd shown at was a no-name place with an owner who'd been lax about promoting Trey. The guy also ended up taking 40 percent of Trey's earnings, so it had been wise for him to move on.

"I don't know how you do it, bro. Doesn't it suck to have people look through your portfolio? Most of them don't know shit about art. They can't see how skilled you are, they don't understand what you're trying to do, and then they have the nerve to turn you down."

Trey smiled his cocky and pretty-fucking-charming smile and said, "It would bother me, until I think how much they'll hate themselves for having turned me down when I get big." Trey took his coffee to the couch, sat, and picked up my yet-to-be-opened *LA Weekly*. I grabbed a bottle of water, took it back to my desk, and went right back to work.

Trey had an hour or so before the galleries opened, at ten. Having him here didn't interrupt my work in the least; in fact, it was a monotony break in a lot of ways. Sometimes knowing another person was around was soothing, especially if it was someone as low key as Trey.

After our talk last night, and my weird sensation of time travel or whatever it'd been, I'd grown curious about Trey's upbringing and wanted to know more. Careful not to come on too strong, I started by asking questions about his being biracial.

"It's weird you having a white mom, dude. I wouldn't have known." I held my pen away from the table and shook it carefully to get the ink to travel to the tip before bringing it to paper. Touching the tip lightly onto the edge of a pebble that needed darkening, I began the tap, tap, tapping motion that marked my stippling work.

"I was used to it. Duffy raised me after Dad left. It wasn't until other kids came over and started asking if I was adopted that I figured I was different."

Without much prompting, Trey began to talk, and I listened while working on my drawing, allowing his voice, his rhythmic cadence, and deep tones to calm me. Just like when I'd been on the phone with him the night before, his doing all the talking was the perfect background to my somewhat tedious work.

"Duffy was married to a white guy before she met my dad. It was weird,'cause I had an all-white half sister."

I didn't even know he had siblings.

"I didn't really like her at first. Trish was all white, not mixed like me, and she was treated ten times better by Duffy's side of the family—the *white* side."

Since I was at my desk with my back to him, I couldn't see Trey's expression, but I could hear him shift on the sofa. I heard him turn the page of the newspaper and set his mug down on the coffee table. I also thought I could hear the resentment in his tone.

My work was flowing now that he was here and doing all the talking. Each point I made on the paper felt automatic and effortless. At times, for split seconds, it almost felt as if it wasn't me doing the work but something inside of me.

"Fuck, the Murphys were nice enough to me, but they spoiled Trish. She got invited over more, she got more shit at Christmas, stuff like that."

When the next vision or hallucination came, I was darkening the pebbles surrounding the tall grasses on the shore of the lake. The pebbles were nothing more than a collection of dots formed in a minute circle with clusters of dots on one side to indicate shadow, but as I drew them, one after the other, my heart began to race.

For no reason I could think of, my heart flipped inside my chest like a fish yanked out of water, and a chill ran up my spine. For a second I wondered if I was having a freak heart attack at twenty-six. I held my pen aside to avoid a spill, and did what I'd done the night before: took a few slow breaths.

Trey went on talking, and I was glad his back was to me. "Trish was cute; she was blonde and bubbly and everyone liked being around her. I was the obvious—nearly literal—black sheep of the family."

Then the strangest thing started happening to my sight. At first I thought there was something wrong with my eyes when my surroundings appeared to move, then roll, then visually dissolve. I tried to focus and shake the illusion but couldn't. The whitewashed brick walls I faced and the window to my left seemed to shiver, liquefy, and then form into an outside space. I heard Trey laugh, somewhere back in my apartment, which was weird, because I wasn't there anymore. I was somewhere else.

Suddenly, and without the chance to acclimate, I found myself in a large backyard. Blotches or pixels of color blended together into images, and I watched helplessly as the millions of gradients of blue came together to form a long, rectangular swimming pool and the nearly cloudless sky above. The greys and whites blended to form the few clouds. The greens combined to form an expanse of lawn, as well as the cypress trees lined up like sentinels that flanked the pool. All these colors, with millions, if not billions of others, joined to create the image of the backyard I stood in. The best way to describe how I went from one visual reality to the other is to imagine a computer generating an image, one pixel at a time. But this visual transformation occurred in an instant—so quickly that I could have missed the entire phenomenon with an extended blink.

Just as the image formed, the summery smell of chlorine and newly cut grass rushed at me in a warm breeze. As I took in my new surroundings, I noticed Trey standing just a few feet away from me on the edge of the lawn where the flagstone surrounding the pool began. His focus was on a lounge chair near the pool, but he didn't seem to see me, even though I stood next to him. The real Trey, who was back in my apartment, was talking, and yet I was too engaged in my new surroundings to listen or pay attention to what he said.

The Trey in this vision looked older than the one in the first vision. He looked to be in his late teens if not older. Like I said, he was staring at a lounger by the pool, so I followed his hard gaze and saw that his attention was on a blonde chick wearing a swimsuit and reclined on the lounger.

He stood to the right of her and behind the headrest of where she lay. From my vantage point, I could see she was completely unaware of him and very much asleep. He slowly walked closer to her and bent down to crouch a little. Again I heard nothing during the vision but my racing heart and Trey still talking somewhere back home, just as clearly as when I'd been at my desk.

"It was weird," Trey was saying back at my place. "She lived with us less than half the time, the rest with her lawyer dad. He gave her stuff to shut her up, so she wouldn't complain about the divorce. She wasn't mean really, but she was pretty manipulative and could be a bitch sometimes. Mom felt sorry for her and bought into her bullshit. If Trish thought Mom should do something, buy something, or fucking paint the house pink, she would."

The Trey in the vision kneeled down slowly next to the girl on the lounger and craned his neck to smell her. I wondered what he was doing, since no matter how I looked at it, it was a weird thing to do—sneak up and smell someone like that.

"We had fun too, I guess. We put on parties at her dad's house. Dude, he had a massive pool. This one time, her friends were over and we were all swimming and shit. Her dad had gone off on a date, so it was just me, Trish, and about twelve other kids. This one dude brought a bottle of vodka, and one of the girls had F Fuck, we got hammered."

As he talked about the party, and while I stood in a yard I'd never seen before, my heart continued to race just like it would if I was jogging or climbing stairs. No matter what I did, there was no stopping my heart from its frantic reaction to the vision. I wondered again if I was having palpitations or the beginnings of an attack.

But something was different this time. The vision I was having was not matching up to Trey's telling. In this vision, Trey was still crouched next to the girl on the lounger and reaching to touch her hair. I saw no party, no other people, just Trey and the girl.

"The thing is, I can't remember any of her friends' names. This one chick was pretty hot, dude. We went out a few times after that. She was like four years older than me."

Then my sight and the vision went black. But as my eyes got used to the darkness, the contours of a room began to take shape and concrete walls formed, pixel by pixel. The more I could see and make out, the more I realized I was in a basement or maybe a garage.

"So out of nowhere, this one chick takes off her swimsuit, and so another chick did too, and then one of the dudes did. Things were getting pretty wild, and Trish kept wanting them to leave, you know, before her dad got home, because she wasn't allowed to have people over."

Trey went on telling his story, and I listened while standing in a strange dark room I'd never been in before. I was scared, I wanted to get the hell out, but I couldn't move. There was nothing for me to do but try to relax.

"The more she asked them to leave, the more they ignored her. I was no help—fuck, ask a hot naked chick to leave?" I heard Trey chuckle, way back in the real world.

When I turned to look behind me, in the dark clammy basement, I saw Trey covered in sweat and his eyes clamped shut while he grimaced hard, like he was making a huge effort.

"It also was the first time I took ecstasy, and, dude...have you dropped E?" The real-time Trey asked me, but I couldn't speak; I couldn't answer. I was staring at the Trey in my vision, who held a shiny metal baseball bat high above his head.

"I got totally horny and shit, which was nothin' new for me, but the colors, the water in the pool looked...it was like fluorescent, you know? A bright fluorescent blue...Shit was cool."

Half listening to the real Trey back home, I watched the drenched Trey in my vision clench his teeth, raise the baseball bat up behind his head, and slam it down onto the ground. There was no sound. I couldn't hear anything, nor could I see what was on the floor in front of him, the thing he was so focused on smashing.

The more Trey talked about the party, the more incongruent I realized my vision was. His words didn't match my vision at all. I wasn't seeing any of it—no naked hot chicks, no bottle of vodka, no pool, just Trey's face and upper body as he continued to obliterate some unseen object with an aluminum baseball bat.

The smell had changed too; gone was the fresh summery smell; the only smell now was a mixture of motor oil and something dank and metallic. Even Trey's clothes looked different than before; they were drenched, and darkened by moisture.

He raised the bat above his head again, and I noticed it was covered in something wet, but in the dimness I couldn't really tell what it was. When he brought it downward again, my whole body jumped involuntarily, and it took me a second to realize why—this time I could hear, this time I heard a thump.

It was intense, this sudden ability to hear sounds in the vision, and they all jumped out at me at once: I heard Trey's heavy breathing, the bat hitting something thick and soft, and a low, almost indecipherable moan. The moan was odd, so primal I wondered if he was killing a dog or some other animal. When he brought the bat up again and drove it down toward his intended target, I heard the thump again, but this time it sounded wet and was followed by a crack.

Trey opened his eyes and looked down at the floor in front of him. He just stood there panting as he stared down at it. Then I saw it, too. I saw a mound covered in a dark, sticky-looking wetness, but I knew right away it was too big to be anything but human.

It wasn't easy to make out features in the dim space, and since blood looks black in the dark, I couldn't be sure it was blood that covered the mass on the concrete floor. Whatever it was looked wet but thick, more like dark syrup than anything that came from a body. Without more light to distinguish color, I couldn't be sure. But the harder I focused, the more things I could identify. When I saw the still-dry blonde hair surrounding what had been a face, I knew it was, or had been, a girl. The skin that wasn't darkened by blood was pale and white, so white it looked artificial, like plastic.

But the thing I couldn't make sense of was the area where the mouth would have been. Something was wrong. There looked to be a thick black thread running vertically over the lips...*What was that?*

I forced myself to look closer at the smashed and bloody mouth, to try to decipher what the black cord-like material was. Then my stomach turned, and I felt hot vomit gathering in my throat…when I realized the lips had been stitched shut.

There was no sign of a nose, no sign of eyes, and above the mouth there was just bone. It had an ear, or what looked like part of an ear torn away from the side of the head. The rest of the head was covered in a matted, bloodied mess of hair with a little of the blonde still visible.

Even though the whole thing was a mess, and no real face was left, the body was still intact. Now that my eyes had adjusted, the small, slim contour of a young woman's body was beginning to take form. If it hadn't been for her small breasts, and pubic hair, she could've passed for a child.The small wrists and legs looked to have been tied and wrapped with duct tape. Aside from her head, and the cuts and scratches on her hands, the rest of her body looked normal.

"The thing is, I started to really like Trish that day, you know? It was like we were friends for once," Trey continued in an easygoing way, a tone that didn't match the horror of my vision. As much as I wanted to scream at the Trey in the vision, as much as I wanted to yell out for him to stop, I was paralyzed.

Then I noticed Trey bend down and remove something from the body. He took it from her and carried it away. When I was able to focus better, I saw he was turning a pink cell phone in his hand, sort of looking at it like he'd never seen it before. Then he stuck it in his front pocket, stood above the body, and cocked his head as he looked down at it for a bit, like he was taking in the details of his handiwork.

All I could do was stand there in a strange, unfamiliar dark basement/ garage in a weird, sleep-like shock. *What was happening to me?* I tried really hard to wake out of the vision or look somewhere else in the room, but I couldn't look away from my friend and the grisly mess on the floor. For some fucked-up reason, I wanted to find her eyes, but it was too dark for that.

In my head I frantically repeated, "This isn't real, this isn't real, this isn't real…" because there was nothing else I knew to do. Repeating the phrase, as useless as it seemed, at least made me feel in control of my sanity.

Then the strangest part of it all happened. The Trey in the vision turned his head and looked right at me like he saw me. My heart jumped in my chest while he stared into my eyes, and I wished the whole time I could look away. But his stare was hard—so focused, it was impossible to break. Then he said, "Hey, man, you there?" His voice was shaky and sounded different. He looked too calm; he sounded too calm. I wanted to yell out and couldn't. I wanted to say, "Fuck, man, there's a dead girl…"

"Dude, you there?"

This time I heard him back in my apartment, back in real time. I blinked and looked around, realizing it was over. I was back home. I could have cried with the relief, but I managed to keep my cool. After all, Trey was a few feet away. I nodded and assured myself all was cool now that I was back home.

After a few beats, I was finally able to speak. "Yeah, sorry, dude. Listen, I'm wiped out. Was up late last night."

I sat back from my desk and turned to see Trey looking up at me from the couch. He got up, stretched, and took his cup back to the kitchen. I slowly stood up and was surprised by how little my equilibrium had been effected, how easily I was back to normal.

Trey walked toward the door and turned. "Gotta head off, show my wares. See you at Craig's."

"Yeah, later." My voice sounded shaky and worn out, even to me.

After the door closed behind him, I sat on the couch, hoping to make sense of what had happened, of what I'd just seen. Fuck, had Trey really killed someone? Everything in the first vision had turned out to be accurate, so did that mean this vision was accurate too? Well, no, I convinced myself, since this time the story Trey told, of the pool party, was nothing like the vision, not at all.

I tried to convince myself that everything I'd seen in this last weird trip was bogus. Sure, the first visions matched up almost exactly to what Trey had said, but this last one didn't. Even so, this vision left a mark, because, hard as I tried, I couldn't get the picture of the mutilated girl, or the blood-soaked hair, out of my mind.

I didn't know it yet, but starting from the phone call the night before, everything in my life would change. When I look back at how it all began and what led to my own personal transformation from a pretty regular guy to someone I no longer recognized, that first phone call marks the beginning.

Awaiting me was a strange journey driven by my obsession to decipher the inexplicable events I witnessed during those visions and the visions that would follow. Little did I know they would grow worse and impossibly realistic. In time, and against my will, I would get sucked into another world, in which everything I saw led to clues that would, in time, be substantiated by reality.

The more visions I had, the more clues there were. Most of the time, it would be like solving a puzzle where the clues only came in dreams. But the dreams—no more than unpredictable moments of semiconsciousness—ended just as capriciously as they came.

Looking back now, it's easier for me to see where I went wrong, easier to spot clues I might've missed. But then, we all know how undeniably pedantic hindsight can be.

SECOND STITCH

WHILE DRIVING TO CRAIG'S PARTY, I began to wonder how I was going to approach Trey. All the shit I'd seen in the visions was bothering me. It had all seemed so real. Sure, I tried convincing myself that it was my whacked-out imagination, but it was getting harder to believe it was only in my head.

By the time I parked my car and walked up to the condo where Craig lived, I was feeling better. Craig's invitation said the party was by the pool in the recreation area of the building, so I followed the signs until I found it.

As I approached the gate leading to the pool, the smell of the BBQ got stronger, the music got louder, and the long peal of some chick's laughter helped me forget the image of the battered girl from the vision. Once I got to the pool and saw a bunch of people I knew from the Art Center, including Kyle, who was talking to Craig as he flipped some burgers, I was back to normal. Kyle looked up at me and raised his beer in greeting.

"Hey, man, it's good to see you," Craig said and smiled, while he used a spatula to flatten a burger. "Heard you left Continental Graphics."

Kyle handed me a beer, which I took.

"Yeah, I kinda had to," I answered. "The pay sucked, and Jay, the dude who owned it, was crazy as shit and—"

Kyle laughed. "I've heard about this guy, he's creepy with chicks too."

I used the interruption to swig from my beer before going on. "He was that, but it was the cigarette smoke that got me in the end. Fuck, this guy ignored all smoking ordinances, smoked all day, shit got in my clothes, in my hair, it was sick."

Craig was interested in my freelance gig. He'd been the only one to asked a shitload of questions when I first told everyone I was considering it. "So is it tough on your own? Wish I had the balls to do that, but I'd be scared shitless," he admitted.

Kyle broke in. "It's different for you, bro. You got an ex and a kid. Being on your own is different."

"That's true," I said. "Having a kid would be hard. No way could I drop my insurance or the steady income. It helped that I put money away and already had a client lined up. I'm working on a proposal now, so it's looking good so far."

I'd seen Trey inside the rec room while I'd been talking to Kyle and Craig. He was sitting on a couch, his arm draped behind some pink-haired chick who looked way too young for him. He must have seen me, but he was either too busy or too into his groove to move from his perch. The thing was, I felt really nervous about heading over to him. This intense, panicky feeling suddenly overcame me, and I had to do everything in my power to chill, so I avoided him.

Just then I saw Sophie, an old friend from work, sitting by herself. Glad to have an excuse to avoid Trey, I headed over to join her.

"Boy, do I miss having you around," Sophie said as I approached her with a beer in one hand and my other dragging a chair behind me.

"No one to mess with, is there?" I said. Sophie and me were big on messing around and keeping the mood light at work. She'd been the one reason I'd stayed on so long.

"No, it sucks. So I tried getting Raj into Reddit, and he goes—and I'm not exaggerating—he goes, 'So references to masturbation, pictures of tile cracks that look like Che, or people doing otherwise dangerous things are funny to you?' And I just stared at him because, *really?*"

I laughed because I could totally picture Sophie being stunned into disbelief. I knew Raj and knew he wouldn't find social online sites entertaining in the least. "So frankly, Sophie, you're alone now..."

She swallowed from her beer and said, "It's just me and the nicotine." Sophie gestured behind her, toward the rec room where Trey was now making out with the chick. "Looks like your buddy isn't too particular," she said sarcastically.

"One thing about Trey: when he doesn't have a girlfriend, he gets stupid. Do you know who she is?"

"All I know is she's a freshman at UCLA, a sociology major. Craig's old roommate used to be her boyfriend. From the looks of it, Trey is her next."

I looked back to where Trey sat with the girl. They weren't making out anymore, just talking with their heads really close. And when Trey saw me, he smiled a cocky smile I knew too well. There was no way he would get caught up with this one; I knew Trey was promiscuous, but he wasn't about to get into a relationship so soon after having broken up with Megan.

"Yeah, I don't think so. Not his type."

The night went by pretty fast, and by the time I got up to say my good-byes to Craig, I realized I'd not spoken to Trey at all. On the way back to my car, I wondered why I'd felt so ill at ease seeing him there. Why had I gone out of my way to avoid my best friend? There was only one reason I could think of: the vision. The vision of Trey beating the girl had done something to alter my feelings for my friend, and it would take time for me to shake it.

A few days went by. I stuck to finishing my illustrations, cleaning up, and reworking the final four I'd picked to show at the presentation later that week. Normally when working on a new project, I would keep my apartment quiet so that I could concentrate on my work. There's a nervous tension involved in courting a new client, and making sure the work is pristine is a big part of dealing with the stress.

But after the weird visions, especially the last one, working in silence was intolerable if not impossible. The only way I could stop the images of the bloody girl or Trey's face from returning was to crank up the music to drown out my thoughts.

Since I was used to working in silence, the music was annoying at first. But the more I listened and let the music guide my imagination, the more the memory of the girl regressed into the back of my mind. Eventually the loud music helped me work faster, and somehow I ended up finishing the proposals earlier than I'd planned.

When I called T&T Associates, Tina answered the phone. She always answered her own phones, and I began to wonder just how big her company was.

"Hi, Tina. I've got four pretty cool proposals I'd like to show you."

I heard her laugh. "That is *so* Art Center of you! Man, you guys come out of that place like pros. I didn't expect to see anything for another couple of weeks."

She paused, and I was about to ask what her schedule was when she said, "You free today? I'm here, so bring it on."

The reality was, I needed the money. I still had savings, but I didn't want to eat away at my stashed money if I didn't need to. If Tina liked and went with one of my illustration concepts, I'd be getting 50 percent up front, and I'd be ahead of the game.

"Cool. I'll be over before lunch, then, depending on traffic."

While driving to Tina's offices in Santa Monica, I played NPR loudly, again as a way of blocking out thoughts of the dead girl. Every time a thought or an image sneaked into my consciousness, I'd focus on every word the interviewer said as if my life depended on it. It took effort, but it worked at distracting myself from reseeing what lay on that concrete floor.

I hadn't seen Trey since the party, and that seemed to have helped with the visions. I'd not had any new ones since. A big part of me wondered if staying away from him had helped stop them—if maybe talking to Trey or seeing him was what brought the hallucinations on.

Once I got off the Fifth Street exit, I followed the GPS voice commands that guided me through a series of turns, until the downtown commercial section became a quaint residential neighborhood. Oddly enough—but not so odd for LA—Tina's offices turned out to be nothing more than a small one-story bungalow on a hip street.

After finding a rare parking spot a few houses away, I grabbed my portfolio and walked up to the house. Tina was standing on the porch of her nicely tended bungalow that had a wild garden in place of a lawn—a mixture of aqua-colored succulents, light green agaves, and the bright purples of a blooming Mexican sage.

"Nice workplace you got here, Tina." I walked up the few short stairs onto the porch and shook her outstretched hand.

Tina smiled and held the door open. "Welcome to my life. I work here, live here, raise kids here...oh, and I cook here, too."

Tina was cute in a short, compact, get-stuff-done sort of way. She laughed and gestured for me to enter. Once inside, I stood in her living room holding my portfolio to my side until she walked past me and headed toward the dinning room table. "Over here is fine. There's coffee, tea, and water behind me. Grab whatever you want."

She watched as I pulled out each illustration proposal to set on the table. "Why don't you lay them this way?" She gestured, indicating how best to lay my pages, before turning to grab two bottles of water from the buffet behind her. Tina set one before me and took the other for herself.

"So the publisher, the guy I mentioned in my e-mail?" Tina sat and scooted her chair closer to the table edge. She looked up at me, as if waiting for me to acknowledge her before continuing. "As you know, he wants the art to look organic, hand drawn, nothing slick to go with the magazine article. And he wants to use the same imagery for the book. The reason I tell you this is, the book will mean a lot more work for you."

I'd been standing while spreading out each proposal on the table in front of her. I pulled out a chair and sat across from Tina, then did my best not to sound too eager when I said, "Well, let's hope one of these works then."

While Tina looked through my drawings, I became nervous that the dead girl's image would rush back into my mind. Finding some way to keep the memory of her prone and bloody mass from creeping back, suddenly became my only focus.

I tried distracting myself by closely studying my surroundings. Taking in details like the wood grain on the surface of the dining table, the arts-and-crafts-style furniture in her living room, and the various kid toys scattered on the floor became vitally important. When I'd studied everything inside her house, I turned my attention outside the window at her garden, at the power lines draped from pole to pole, at the parked cars shinning in the sun. Finally, I looked back at my drawing, joining Tina, whose attention was aimed at the lake I'd drawn.

Maybe my guard was down, maybe I'd relaxed too much, because no matter where I looked this time, all I saw was the bloodied hair surrounding the crushed and mangled face on the floor of the dark room. Several beads of cold sweat dripped down my side, and I wondered if Tina could hear my heart pounding. Stiffening in my seat, I tried to look away from my drawing, but before I did, I saw a small strange rock I'd not seen before, this one uncannily resembling the girl's partially severed ear.

"Ooooh, I like this. I like this one a lot." Tina held up the lake drawing, the one I'd been working on when the first and second visions had hit.

She leaned in to get a closer look at the lake, the two curled and scraggly-looking trees off in the distance, and the San Gabriel Mountains hugging the scenery from behind. She leaned in closer to admire the texture created by the multitude of rocks I'd drawn along the lakeshore.

"Oh, this look is a definite must…love these rocks." She set the drawing down on the table and pointed to the rocks. I followed her finger as she outlined the curious curve of the shore and said, "How long did this take you? That's a ton of rocks—so much detail."

Like I said, I was following her finger, taking in all the rocks I'd so meticulously drawn, but I didn't see rocks anymore. I saw grimacing faces, some with mouths partly open as if in midgroan, some had eyes raised as if looking at the sky with mostly whites showing, and one with black, yarn-like stitches sealing its mouth closed. My heart started racing all on its own, and the familiar panicky feeling of losing consciousness nudged at me.

The only thing I could think to do was take deep breaths while hoping I wasn't hit by a vision right in front of a potential client. More drops of perspiration ran down my side, just under my shirt, mercifully away from Tina's view.

When I glanced up, Tina was staring at me in a weird, expectant way. And it hit me—I'd not answered her question. "Oh, how long? Sorry, it's tough to say. You know how time totally disappears when you're doing something like this. I'd say twenty hours tops, but more after I scan and really clean the drawings up."

Although Tina nodded and smiled at my response, her glance lingered on me a bit longer than normal. It was hard to put my finger on it, but I got the distinct sense she'd grown wary of me or picked up on my discomfort.

But I managed to keep my cool as best I could for the rest of the meeting. By the time I left, with a deal sealed for ten drawings, I was drenched in sweat and happy to be back in my car.

When I started the engine, I cranked up the air conditioning to the highest level and let the cold air cool and dry me off. My phone began to vibrate and hum on top of my portfolio. When I glanced at the screen and read Trey's name, I answered, even though a part of me wanted to avoid him altogether.

In the long run, avoiding Trey just because of my fucked-up visions would only make things worse. What I needed was to be with him. Spending time with him was the only way I could think to dispel the visions.

"Hey, you wanna get a burger at Smitt's?" Trey asked right off.

"Yeah, I could use a beer and a burger."

"I'm a block away. I'll get us a table and wait for you out front." Trey hung up, and I began to feel better.

I figured I'd tell him my good news when I saw him. Getting the contract with Tina's firm was a big deal, and once I got paid in full, it would bring in more money than I'd made working for two months at Universal Graphics.

With one deal under my belt, I had a lot to be happy about, and I suddenly felt like celebrating. Striking out on my own was looking to be a good thing.

Trey was sitting outside when I got to Smitt's. He looked relaxed and happy, happier than I'd seen him since he'd broken up with Megan. Maybe a couple of wild nights with pink-hair had helped.

We talked about all kinds of stuff while we waited for our food and drank our first beers. Then Trey came right out and said, "Listen, all that shit with my mom…it's all in the past, you know?"

I thought about all of my own family issues and smiled. "It's called growing up, dude." I smirked and waited to see if he'd say anything more about Trish.

The thing was, since I'd rushed to get off the phone with Trey that first night, I'd not asked about where Trish was now. I really wanted to know, and had even considered calling him back that night to ask. So I chose my words carefully when I finally asked, not wanting to sound as freaked out as I was.

"What, ah, what ever happened to Trish anyway? Do you guys talk?"

Just then our waitress came out with our burgers. It felt like forever as she set down our plates and asked if we wanted anything else, all while I waited impatiently for her to leave.

Trey exhaled long and hard and stared at his plate before answering. His brown eyes seemed stern as he focused, as if the thing he was going to say required huge effort. When he did speak, his voice sounded much different; it sounded calm, but with a weird modulating pitch, which was how he sounded when something bothered him.

"Trisha ran off; she just took some of her stuff and disappeared. Mom reported it, and there was this half-assed local investigation, but we never saw or heard from her again. Mom just got one last good-bye, fuck-you text from her the day she left, and that was it."

I didn't know what to say. I didn't expect to hear that. I guess I'd imagined she'd be married with kids and living somewhere nice. I took a bite from my burger to cover up my confusion and waited for Trey to say more.

He cleared his throat and looked sad when he added, "I still remember that pink phone cover. I got it for her at one of those mall stands…She actually used it, too. It was the only thing I ever gave her she liked."

Pink phone. I swallowed my burger, almost choking on it, remembering Trey standing over the mangled body while holding a pink phone. All sorts of thoughts raced through my mind. My heart started its wild beating, so I tried to calm myself by sipping from my beer.

"The thing is, once Trish left, patching things up with Duffy hasn't been going so well. Let's just say she has her way of looking at things that I don't agree with."

The next thing I said came out before I could think it through. "Yeah, I've heard death either separates families or brings them closer."

Then Trey jumped in, sounding like regular Trey again. "Well, we don't know if she's dead. The investigators said we shouldn't get our hopes up, *but* since there was no body..."

Here Trey stopped, and looked away briefly before continuing. "They said that we could never know, she might just show up one day. We just don't know."

Fuck, I felt like shit now. I shouldn't have said that. It was true, kids ran away all the time. Still, though, it was too perfect, too clean. Trish running off, never to be seen again, was precisely what a guilty guy would say.

After a while, I paid the bill and made up some excuse for leaving. I needed to think things out.

When I got back to the apartment, I grabbed a soda and stood by the big window to look outside. Being with Trey hadn't made me feel any better. In fact, it was hard not to be suspicious of him. As I took in the quiet residential street outside, it struck me how benign and harmless everything looked, how easily the street could pass for a place where only good, upstanding people lived. Out walking her small black dog was tiny and harmless Katherine, the old Russian lady who lived in the cottage on the corner. There was the familiar murmur of Stan's TV from the apartment downstairs. And there, flashing past, was a white SUV with a mom and her kids tucked inside. It was normal stuff. All of it appeared right.

Those were the things I could see. What bothered me were the things I couldn't see, like the married guy who raped women in alleys, or the dog who wagged his tail even though his master beat him, or the kid who brewed with hate until the day he shot up a movie theater. There was so much we didn't see and couldn't know. *Fuck, how much bad shit was happening now?* Someone somewhere was being hurt or tortured, and no one would know. How could things look so benign on the outside when so much hidden crap was going on?

Either way, thinking too much about it wasn't going to solve anything. I turned away from the window, dropped onto the couch, and flipped on the TV. Clicking aimlessly, I searched channels for something to take me away from what was becoming an obsession. After a few minutes, I heard my cell humming on the kitchen counter but didn't give it much thought. Later, when I got up to check it, I was surprised to see there was a text from Rachel.

Rachel and I had hooked up a few times, and although I really liked hanging out with her, I didn't have a desire to spend all my time with her. When it became clear she wanted a relationship and I didn't, not with her anyway, we broke up.

It was a little weird hearing from her now. It'd been like eight months since I'd seen her, so when I read her text saying she was in the neighborhood and wanted to stop by. I texted back and said sure.

It didn't take her long. I heard her footsteps running up the stairs to my door maybe ten minutes later. I'd left the front door open and was cleaning up a bit when she called from the threshold. "Don't go flattering yourself thinking I'm stalking you. I really just wanted to say hi, see how things were with you…"

Not even in the door, and Rachel was at it. "Man, Rache, you're an explanation machine, aren't you?"

I handed her a beer before heading to the couch with mine, slapping the seat next to me for her to sit, but she just stood there. She'd gained some weight since I'd last seen her, cut her hair and dyed it redder, but she still looked good. Rache had a freckled-face wholesome look to her—the type of look that made people trust her right off. She took a swig from her beer, plopped next to me on the couch, shook her head, and said, "I just missed this…"

"Me too." I didn't need her to explain. I knew what she meant. I missed our easy hanging out too. Not that the sex hadn't been good.

"So…what's going on with you these days?" Rache asked me cautiously, probably wondering if I was seeing anyone else, which I wasn't.

"I'm good, you know. I got the illustration gig up and working…"

By now I was really happy she'd come over. Maybe, if I used the right words, I could tell her about my visions. Hell, I needed to tell someone; carrying these fucked-up images around was taking its toll on me. They were eating away at my moods, my sanity, my friendship with Trey, *everything*. So after we'd had a few beers, I gave it a go, knowing that really I had nothing to lose, because they were just visions, right?

I'd been studying her face for any doubt while I told her about the girl being beaten, about watching Trey doing it, and was relieved not to see any. If anything, Rache was more animated and interested than I'd ever seen her.

After I'd finished, she sat up on the couch and faced me. "Wow, this is fucked up. This is some really scary, hole-yourself-up-in-an-asylum type of shit. You saw Trey? Holding the baseball bat?"

I swigged from my beer and nodded. "That place we were in was creepy as fuck. It was like a basement or something, and I could smell things."

"Yeah, the pool part wasn't so bad, but the basement..." Rache shivered and set her beer down on the coffee table.

"He stood over her body when he was done, looking down at it like he was satisfied. Shit, Rache, I just want to forget all of it, you know? But then I wonder why I saw it in the first place. Am I supposed to do something?"

Rachel let this sink in before going on. "Okay, first, just because you're having visions doesn't mean shit. You can't base real life on visions or hallucinations, but...man, these seem so right on, so accurate. Maybe you're having some sort of psychic phase, you know? Like some people can, like, totally become bipolar in their twenties. It goes away, but it sure messes them up for a few years. The same could be happening to you with the ability to see things—see them as they really are...or were."

My feet were up on the coffee table, and I was feeling pretty relaxed, maybe a little buzzed from all the beer, but not unable to think straight. I wondered why I hadn't tried calling Rache before; it felt good telling someone all of this.

"So, Rache, don't hold back, okay? What do you think about it all? You think maybe I'm psychic, and Trey is a crazed killer who just happens to look and act totally normal?"

She was on her fourth beer by now, her feet up next to mine on the table. She was looking straight ahead, probably trying to make sense of everything I'd described. So I gave her time. We sat without saying much for a while, then Rache suddenly turned to me as if with a revelation.

"You know what I really think?" she asked, and I nodded, because, yes, I really wanted to know what someone else—someone not plagued by these visions—thought.

"I think you have to ask yourself, 'Am I willing to call the police to report this?' Because if all of this was really real, the first thing you would do would be to call the police."

That made sense. Rache was right. If I really believed Trey had killed someone, no matter how long ago, I'd be driven to call the cops. But I hadn't been. Maybe, deep down, I didn't believe what I'd seen was real.

"Fuck, Rache, that's right. The thought never even entered my mind."

Rache nudged my foot with hers and chuckled. "I think our minds are pretty powerful things. If you thought Trey had killed her, like in real life, you would have called to report it, even if the baseball bat and the pink cell phone cover were the only hard evidence. Somehow your brain knows the visions are just that—visions. Besides, I don't think Trey is capable."

"I get that. It makes total sense…I can't believe I never thought of that."

"Hey, it helps having friends with psych degrees, doesn't it?" Rache asked in her much-too-cute way.

By the time Rachel left that night, I was feeling better than I'd felt in a long time. Part of it was because after months of not seeing her I'd missed the friendship we'd had. Being with her had felt totally normal and relaxed, and even though we could never get into a relationship again, I hoped we could at least hang out every now and then.

Later, as I lay in bed, some of the things Trey told me came back. That Trish had simply vanished, left her family and friends without a trace, was likely. I'd read about a lot people who did that—left everything and everyone behind and then showed up years later without notice.

No matter what, I was grateful Rachel had called and we'd reconnected. She could prove to be a great person for me to vent to. She could be the one hold I had on reality, should I begin to doubt myself again.

But as I went back and thought of all she'd said, I suddenly remembered her mentioning the baseball bat, which I'd told her about, and then the cell phone, which I hadn't. I distinctly remembered *not* mentioning the pink cell. I remembered thinking that it was too much detail to go into.

I went over our talk to make sure I hadn't mentioned it, and after a bit, I began to doubt myself. Maybe I *had* said something and totally forgot; after all, I'd had six beers on an empty stomach. Hell, I must've mentioned the pink cell; how else would Rache know about it? I made a mental note to call her the next day and ask.

On a happier note, I was looking forward to meeting up with Trey at Barney's the next day—even more so now that Rache had shed logic on the whole vision issue. Just like we'd been doing for years, I'd meet up with Trey without any weird doubts looming, and soon I'd forget all about the pictures in my head and feel better. Maybe after a couple of beers I could tell him about the visions, and hell, maybe we'd laugh about them.

THIRD STITCH

"*Sewing through someone's skin the first time is bound to freak you out. Do not wait too long if it's a cadaver—rigor mortis will only make your work tougher.*"

This is what came up when I googled mouth-sewing rituals—a Pandora's box of weird shit. People did this?

There was more: "*Mouths were commonly sewn closed using household materials such as thick string, cord, twine, fencing wire, and yarn. The ritual was performed on the living as punishment. It was performed on the dead who held secrets. It was believed that a sewn mouth prevented secrets from being revealed in the afterlife. Families with prepubescent daughters assured the child's purity, or rather, virginity, by affixing vaginal canals with stitches.*"

The girl's mouth in the vision had been sewn shut. And although her head and face had been mutilated, I clearly saw the thick, black cord woven tightly through distinct holes in her lips.

I couldn't read anymore. I closed the page, letting the gruesome world of ritualistic practices dematerialize back into the virtual world it came from.

Besides, I had work to do. I clicked back onto the first completed illustration I was about to forward to Tina and gave it a final check. As I scanned the document, my eyes darted to the one rock, the small one lying near the black shore of the lake. Its mangled, grimace-like expression still resembled the mashed face of the girl in the basement; its mouth still appeared sewn shut.

It was strange how a few turns of my pen, meant to draw a shaded river rock, instead created what looked like a sewn mouth; how the muddied prairie grass around it became tangled, wet hair.

After writing Tina a quick note, I took one last look at the attachment and clicked send.

With my first illustration under my belt and off to my new client, I was feeling pretty stoked. Since the night was warm, I decided to wait for Trey outside. There were steps in front of the apartment building where I lived, and on evenings like these, when the hot Santa Ana winds were blowing, it was fucking surreal to sit and listen to the wind whip through trees, shake bushes, and howl like it was alive.

It was blowing pretty hard when I got to the steps. Everything that wasn't manmade seemed to shake in the strong gusts. The tiny leaves on the Japanese maple shivered under the streetlight, causing weird shadows to materialize on the sidewalk. They looked like tiny little shivering mouths that gaped open to laugh and smile. It was pretty cool, like a cartoon of some sort, with just the mouths yapping away...until I saw one mouth that wasn't flapping, a mouth with dark stripes like bindings, keeping it from opening. I blinked and was about to get up from the steps to get a closer look, when Trey's voice startled me.

"Dude, what the fuck are you looking at?"

I'd been so distracted I'd not noticed Trey's car drive up. He was leaning over and watching me through the open passenger-side window, not ten feet away from me. He smiled, looking amused while he shook his head. Fuck, I didn't blame him. I must've looked like a dickhead sitting there staring at the ground.

"You on something, artist boy?" Trey teased when I got in the car. In a way, I was grateful. I'd been through some heavy stuff lately, and I welcomed the chance to laugh.

On our way to Barney's I told him about signing the ten-illustration deal with the publishing house. He slapped his steering wheel with genuine happiness and chuckled. "I knew you could do this on your own, dude! Why slave away for some company where you get paid the same no matter how good your work? Congratulations, you deserve it."

"Thanks, man. It feels good." Then it occurred to me to tell him about Rache. I told him about her coming over, but left out what we'd talked about. "It was cool, we hung out, had a few beers, caught up on shit. But we're not back together or anything."

Trey glanced over at me, as if trying to figure out if I really was okay with Rache being back as just a friend. "Cool. So she's back from Denmark? She okay with it—the just being friends thing?"

I recalled hearing that she'd gone to Europe and wondered why she hadn't mentioned it when she'd been over. I was thinking this when I realized I hadn't answered Trey's question. "Yeah, she's cool with it."

We didn't talk much during the short drive, and I wouldn't have noticed until I felt Trey looking at me weird. "Hey, man, are you okay?"

"I'm fine...why? Do I seem like I'm not?"

He glanced my way before turning left into the parking lot across the street from Barney's. Then he said, "You've been different, like something's on your mind."

"I'm fine, really."

Trey pulled into a spot and stopped the car. His gaze lingered on me until I opened my door and got out. The fact was, I was feeling really uncomfortable and not as relaxed as I'd once been around Trey.

As soon as we opened the door to Barney's, the dependably loud and crowded bar welcomed us. Better yet, walking in and finding our regular places at the bar made it feel like old times. The semblance of normalcy, the familiar sites and sounds of the place, coaxed me into a false sense of the regular.

The next thing I decided to do will seem strange. It's difficult to explain why or how it occurred to me, but I made a point to avoid any physical contact with Trey. It wasn't like we touched much anyway, but for some reason— primal instinct or whatever—I avoided touching him. It could be that, deep down, I feared that touching him might prompt a vision, which sounds illogical, given it hadn't set one off in the past, but I hadn't been thinking logically lately anyway.

Jason, who'd tended bar for as long as we'd been coming in, raised his head in greeting from behind the long counter. Without having to ask, he reached for two glasses and began pouring our beers.

"Kept them open for you," Jason said, referring to our stools.

"Thanks, man," I said. Trey, on the other hand, kept quiet. Something was on his mind, but making Trey talk when he didn't want to was never an option.

Trey hesitated before drinking, smiled, turned his glass on the counter absentmindedly, and came out with his news. "I got my own show, man." Suddenly he was smiling big, and he was happy, happier than I'd ever seen him.

"Are you fucking serious? A solo show? Just you?" Here's when I reached out to slap Trey on his back but pulled away right before I made contact, pretending to sweep the hair off my face. It got me a weird look from Jason, who glanced up from wiping a glass.

Trey smiled bigger now, shook his head, and let out a stunned laugh. I was happy for him. Getting a gallery in LA was nearly impossible; getting a solo show as a newbie in the art world just didn't happen. Trey offered more.

"Charlie Webb heard about my series and called me."

"Webb's? You're showing at fucking Webb's? And he called you? Shit, Trey, this is it, dude. You're made, you know that?"

Something was wrong. Trey had dropped his head into his chest, and his shoulders shook. I wasn't sure what was going on. "Hey, man, you okay?"

No answer from Trey, just a nod of his head. When he looked up, his eyes were wet, but still he smiled through the emotion overcoming him. He'd wanted a show more than anything. He'd worked and waited six years for this, so it wasn't a surprise that he was getting emotional. I felt happy for his big win, so I put my hand on his back. *Forgetting.*

Then it happened, with no warning. I saw a long black string of yarn running down the top of the bar right in front of our glasses and continuing down the stretch of counter. My heart began to pound just like it had when the first visions started. As soon as I leaned into the bar to see where the yarn led, I wasn't in Barney's anymore.

I stood in a hallway. No furniture, no pictures, just shiny white floors and white walls. But somehow being in this strange, blank space didn't register as much as the black yarn. My eyes were glued to the curved line of black wool running down the center of the hall. There was a fierce instinct driving me toward it. So I gave in. I followed the yarn until it stopped at an open doorway.

Although I wasn't at Barney's anymore, I still heard Jason talking to Trey back at the bar. "Congratulations, man. When's the show?" It was odd hearing Jason's voice while standing here, wherever I was.

"Six months. I have time to work on new pieces before we hang," Trey answered. He sounded like he was right next to me, so I turned my head to be sure, but all I saw were glaring white walls and shiny white flooring.

"So what's your series about?" Jason again, back at Barney's, where real life was taking place.

The line of yarn appeared to be moving. The closer I got to the door, where it turned at the threshold, the more it jumped, as if someone was pulling on it.

Once at the doorway, the brightness of the room, the whiteness of it all, was such a strain, I had to pause at the threshold to allow my eyes to adjust. Slowly things began to take shape: the edge of a stark white sink, a window with tightly closed Venetian blinds, and folded towels on top of a toilet. Even before my eyes could fully settle, I made out Trey sitting on the edge of the tub. He was holding a ball of black yarn in one hand while he wound the long, loose strand around it.

The Trey in the vision, the one sitting on the edge of the tub, looked up at me and answered Jason back at the bar. "I work in extremes, blacks and whites. The starkness of the two is powerful..."

He kept his gaze on me as he wound the yarn around the ball while speaking in a calm voice. "Love, hate, life, death, clean, and dirty. They maintain integrity when they stand alone, but when you mix them, they're diluted, and you get grey, and grey is dull. People don't like looking at grey things."

Trey, the one in the vision, went back to his winding and began to murmur to himself. I could hear him; I could hear both him and the sounds of the bar. "Grey is dull, grey is dull..." I wanted to shut him up, but no words came. A part of me was still very aware of really being at the bar, not here in this too-white bathroom.

Then I heard a splash and a weird tinkling sound behind Trey. He kept winding his ball rhythmically while I approached the tub. He didn't seem to mind that I stood right next to him, it didn't seem to matter to him that I could see the girl inside the tub. Still alive, but pale and bound, the blonde girl cowered in the bath water. *Was this Trish?*

There were layers of duct tape placed over her mouth, and there was blood seeping through the side where the tape was ripped. Then I saw the ice. Inside the tub, and mixed in with the bath water, was ice, lots of it.

The most pressing part of these visions, what I hope you'll understand, is that I wasn't able to do what I wanted. What I wanted was to pull her out, but I couldn't. Unlike lucid dreaming, where you have will, I was unable to control my actions, and there was no token or code word to get me out.

Her eyes were focused on mine, there was no doubt she was looking right at me, but suddenly she clamped them shut. Was she trying to wipe the image of me away by closing her eyes? Oh fuck, it suddenly occurred to me that she might be afraid I was going to hurt her. I tried to reach out to touch her, to calm her, but I couldn't move. Even so, I saw her flinch and cower away from me just like a panicked animal.

She was naked, and so white that her wet and shiny skin looked like china. Being submerged in all that ice would kill her, and it would be a slow death. She moved again, as if to crawl away from the edge of the tub where I stood, and that's when I saw the roundness of her belly. I'd sketched pregnant women in my live-model drawing classes countless times, so I knew what that bump was. She was pregnant.

Trey didn't look up from his yarn when he started up in a singsong chant. "Grey is dull, grey is dull...." I hadn't noticed that he was bleeding, that his forearms where covered in scratches. One scratch ran up inside his inner arm. It was a deep scratch, the type that would leave a scar.

I thought hard about pulling Trish out of the tub, willing myself to move, but as soon as the thought came, I was back at the bar.

Jason was wiping the counter while listening to Trey's rant. "Grey is dull..."

"Stop it," I said. How I was able to spit this out and sound remotely normal is still a surprise. The one thing on my mind was that Trey's mantra was annoying, and I wanted it to stop.

Trey laughed. He didn't seem bothered by my outburst.

"Sorry, man," I said. "It's annoying as fuck."

My heart thumped and I tried keeping my cool after seeing the girl—who I was sure had to be Trish—alive. Acclimating so fucking fast, from such a violent vision to being back at Barney's, wasn't easy. I couldn't stop my hands from shaking. Two moods seemed to overcome me—rage, aimed at Trey, and fear of what he was capable of.

"No worries. It's meant to be annoying. I thought I'd have my DJ buddy record a track of me saying it for the opening, and I'd have him add some linear music to it."

That's right. He'd been talking about his show. I visualized the white bathroom again, and the black yarn running down the tiled floor. Then, to be sure, I shot a glance down the bar and wasn't surprised the line of black yarn I'd seen so clearly just minutes before was gone.

"I don't know," I said, my voice sounding pretty shaky. "Don't you think other people might get tired of hearing the same thing over and over again?"

Jason laughed. He was pouring beer and looked up. "It'd drive me fucking nuts."

Trey nodded, but insisted, "It'll only be in the background, like percussion, you know, like a drumbeat. I'm playing an old recording of my sister reading her poetry. That'll be what you hear most."

"You mean Trish? The one who disappeared?" I asked as calmly as I could.

Trey didn't look at me, but looked genuinely sad. I knew him, I knew when Trey was being honest, and this sadness was honest.

"She was my *half* sister, and a pretty good poet, so it's sort of an homage to her."

Jason walked off to deliver a beer, but I kept my eyes on Trey, who looked down at his glass. He waited for a while before speaking again.

"There really were good times. When we were kids, she told me her dad had said some shit about me being black. It didn't surprise me. My mom said she left him because he was a dickhead and a total racist. He flipped out when she met my dad and, later, when she had me. It seems Trish was really hurt by her dad not liking me, and even stood up for me."

I wanted to see a picture of her. I wanted to see if she looked like the girl I'd just seen in the tub. "Do you have pictures of her, of Trish?"

Trey looked away, his eyes a deep dark brown. "I might have one stuffed away somewhere, but Duffy has most everything. Had to e-mail her like five times to get those poetry tapes."

He finished his beer before going on. "Duffy and me don't really talk. She's been living with this weird dude in Pasadena for years. They're at Wayne Manor up on the hill. They used to film *Batman* and shit there, remember? Awesome place. I used to housesit, but now I stay away, and that's fine by me."

After the last vision, I was pretty much straining to listen to Trey, and as much as I wanted to know about Trish, I was getting overwhelmed by exhaustion and a need to be alone. It was no surprise I'd also lost my taste for beer. I stood up, settled my tab with Jason, and congratulated Trey on nabbing a solo show. When he asked if I wanted a ride back home, I lied and said I needed the fresh air.

Just before I turned to go, I searched Trey's arms for scars. His forearms were partially covered by his rolled-up sleeves, but no scars or marks were visible.

Later that night, I did all I could to keep myself distracted so the visions wouldn't haunt me. Flipping through hundreds of TV stations, I stopped briefly on an old episode of *Bewitched*, but it only made me feel more anxious when people ganged up on Darren, refusing to believe him after he'd described being on the stand at the Salem witch trials. I knew too well how Darren felt, and though I'd seen this episode tons of times and laughed, this time it was agonizing to watch.

It was frustrating to witness something so real and yet so unlikely. Who could I talk to about the visions? I'd set my hopes on Rache to be a confidante, but she wasn't at my beck and call.

I clicked off the television and headed to bed, even though I sensed sleep wouldn't come easily. Seeing Trish alive, bound, and helpless in that tub without the ability to help her gnawed on me. The book by Paul Auster I'd been so excited about reading before now felt too overwhelming to approach, its dark tones too much like real life.

I'd texted Rache earlier in the day, so I checked my phone to see if she'd responded, but she hadn't. Sleeping was impossible. There was no way of forcing it, so I got up, poured myself a glass of wine, headed to my computer, and set to the meticulous work of cleaning up my illustrations.

I scanned one of the drawings and waited for the image to materialize on the screen. The lake, the grasses, and the countless river rocks appeared. The work of cleaning areas surrounding the lake, the areas that needed defining, amounted to finding minute, smudge-like sections where the ink had bled into the white background. It would take hundreds if not thousands of clicks to clean up and sharpen the edges of my earlier pen work, but the repetitive effort was soothing.

The irony that I was eliminating all greys from my work didn't escape me. As I did so, the rocks began to look even more like faces, all ghostly and focused on me. The one I'd noticed when I'd been at Tina's office, the one with the stitched mouth, stared back at me with a stronger, more desperate determination. The eyes were wider than I remembered; these eyes expressed terror, much like those of the girl in the tub.

Even though I still hadn't determined who the girl in the tub was, I was growing more convinced it was Trish. It struck me then, more than ever before, how much I wanted to know more about her, more about what really happened. Trey was so resolved when he claimed she'd disappeared that I had to accept his side of the story was true. But maybe Duffy would have more. It was the only way to find out if Trey's side of the story was true or just protective bullshit. Hell, Duffy might be the talkative type and offer up all kinds of important information. It was worth a try.

I waited a few days before looking up Duffy's address and phone number in Pasadena and a few days more before calling her to set up my awkward visit to Wayne Manor.

FOURTH STITCH

"*Using an ice pick to preform puncture holes through thicker skin around the mouth makes sewing a mouth easier.*"

Ten. It said it takes ten stitches to get a mouth sewn shut. For some reason, I imagined it would take fewer.

Then I read something new: "*Ice living tissue before puncturing. Icing stiffens live tissue, making puncturing and sewing simpler. Icing also deadens pain.*"

I'd woken up that morning, had cereal, washed it down with instant coffee, and was now at my desk and on the computer. It occurred to me the night before that learning more about sewing rituals might shed light on why someone like Trey might be intrigued by them. The last sentence echoed in my head: "*Icing also deadens pain.*" Was that the reason Trey had placed Trish in an ice-filled tub? To deaden her pain?

Again I'd suffered through a night of unsteady sleep. I awoke to sounds I'd once slept through. A car door closing in the alley, a siren going off in the distance, or a dog's faraway bark pulled me out of sleep. When I had slept, I'd been hounded by odd dreams, dreams where I found myself in strange places with strange people, getting lost on unfamiliar streets. I sensed I was being chased, but didn't have a place to hide. Those dreams were a blur now, but the feeling of them lingered over me like an uncomfortable dread.

With that dreaded sense weighing me down, I kept reading about sewing rituals. There seemed to be quite a few online sites where people had taken the time to research and describe these types of rites, and I wondered about who these people were. Was Trey also obsessed with torturous rituals? Had he also been on sites like these?

My heart started pounding when I remembered the expression on Trey's face as he sat on the edge of that white tub, how calm he'd seemed. The pounding in my chest got worse and began to thump in my ears. I put my head in my hands and covered my ears, but it did nothing. I stood up and walked, hoping that moving around would help, but no. The throbbing got louder and louder, until a sharp pain pierced through my skull and I dropped down to my knees and held my head in my hands.

Then it stopped, and the relief was almost exhilarating. I remained still and embraced the quite for a moment before attempting to stand when, without any warning, I lost consciousness.

When I came to and tried opening my eyes, the intensity of the bright white room forced them shut again. Even so, I'd seen enough to know I was back in the white bathroom, standing in front of the tub.

Trey was there, to my left and hunkered over the tub near Trish's head. Her mouth was stuffed with wet towels, pushing out her lips in an exaggerated way. Then I saw it, one distinct red hole on her upper lip. It looked too clean, too perfectly round, and much bigger than it needed to be to accommodate the thickness of the yarn. The skin surrounding her lips was blue, but the hole itself was red, except for a spot of pinkish-white where Trish's bloody teeth showed through.

The pounding in my ears had come back, and it was loud. It was the only sound I could hear. Gratefully, it drowned out anything Trey might've been saying, and above all it masked the sound of ice clinking in the tub. All I heard was the loud rushing in my ears. *Woosh, woosh, woosh, woosh.*

As Trey bent over her, I could see his lips moving and knew he was talking. He rubbed a chunk of ice roughly over her mouth, but he held something else in his grip, something metal, sharp, and shiny. I tried looking away, but no matter where I looked, no matter if I closed my eyes, the same vision appeared. There was no escaping the scene in the tub.

The pointed metal shaft of the ice pick glinted in the light, catching my attention. Trey took hold of Trish's top lip with one hand, pulled it away from her mouth, and began to bore another hole through it. Trish began to struggle in a frenzied and almost spastic way, her bound feet kicking helplessly in the tub, splashing ice cubes and water all over the place, but it was futile. She was tied up, and Trey was too strong. I saw her round, pregnant belly, and an intense rush of hatred coursed through me. I hated Trey. I hated him now more than ever, and there was no going back.

I knew I was yelling while I stared into Trish's closed eyes. I was frozen, unable to move, and unable to hear myself, but I knew I was yelling. I didn't know what I was yelling until I came out of the vision and was back in my apartment.

"Don't look, Trish. Please don't look." I was crying hard too, harder than I'd cried since I was a kid.

When I opened my eyes I was in my bed and sobbing. *How the fuck had I gotten here from the living room?* I quickly climbed out and went back to the living room. Sitting on the edge of the couch, I looked around, taking deep breaths and trying to picture a beach somewhere, with white sand and turquoise water, but the picture kept dissolving into Trish's awful expression and the raw fear of the moment she'd suffered.

This last vision shook me to my core. All I knew to do was shiver on the couch and try to recover while denying the visions were taking an emotional toll. But it was tough to ignore how loosely my boxers fit, ignore how much my appetite had waned, ignore my low threshold for rage, or deny how erratic my sleep had become.

As much as I tried to stop thinking about Trey, Trish, or the visions, one question nagged at me: Could Trey really have killed his own sister? He'd said there'd been a time when they'd strayed, right before she'd disappeared. Maybe something had happened between them? Maybe it had to do with her being pregnant?

Then I began to wonder how I could stay friends with Trey. Shit, what else didn't I know about him? If he could do that to his own sister, what else was he capable of? It was hard to see him in those visions—a guy I thought I loved—torture someone like that. How was I supposed to be his friend now?

Remembering the relief I'd felt when I'd confided in Rache, I looked to see if she'd answered my text from the night before. The thought of calling was appealing and seemed like a good way to calm myself, so I grabbed the phone and was about to call, when it occurred to me that Rache had a life separate from mine now and maybe I was coming on too strongly. She might get the wrong idea if I called too much. Besides, what could she do except talk me through it?

The thing was, I really needed to talk to somebody. I needed to vent. My world was creeping up on me faster than I could stop it. Besides losing weight and being sleep deprived, something else was going on with me, something harder to pinpoint. I was changing. I wasn't myself. The patience and calm I used to count on as part of who I was, was slipping through my fingers.

I kept losing it in public and found myself doing shit I'd never done before. I was becoming *that guy*. The guy who got pissed when people took too long at the ATM, who flipped you off if you honked your horn, the guy who got bothered by silly shit. None of it seemed important until I attacked a man at the park.

It happened all too quickly. And even though I knew I was losing it and felt like shit while it all happened, nothing could stop me from beating up the poor guy right in front of his kid.

The reason I'd gone to the park in the first place was to get a few pictures of a big oak I wanted to use in a drawing, but as soon as I got there, all I could hear was this whiny kid hollering. He wouldn't let up either, he was on an ear-splitting roll, and it was annoying as shit.

As much as I tried to mantra myself out of it, to tell myself to "Relax... let it go, it's just a kid," the sound of his squealing hounded me. When I finally glanced over to get a look at the kid, I noticed he was maybe five or six years old and sitting on the lawn with his dog. As I watched—now more interested than I should have been—I realized he was not only hollering at his chocolate Lab but also hitting it. The poor dog was blinking, walking backward, and trying to duck the swipes, but the kid managed to get a few hard slaps in.

There was a guy on a cell phone nearby who I assumed was the kid's dad. The dad turned his head away from the phone, called out something to the kid, but went right back to his call, utterly unaware his boy was terrorizing the poor dog. The boy looked up at his dad, waited for him to turn away, and then slugged the dog again. This time I heard the poor Lab whimper.

I couldn't take it anymore so I jogged over, but I stopped when the kid began to wail and cry. It seems he'd hurt his hand on the metal buckle on the dog's collar when he'd hit it. Then, only after hearing his kid's dramatic crying, did the dad finally drop his phone and attend to him.

By now I was close enough to see when the dad pointed a cautionary finger at the Lab in order to scold the poor animal. "Bad dog, Ivan! Bad dog!"

It struck me as wrong and unfair the dog was getting blamed for the bratty kid's behavior, so I ran to the guy to explain. "Hey, man, it's not the dog's fault, your kid was hitting him pretty hard."

But the guy ignored me. I was standing right in front of him, so I knew he could fucking hear me, but he pretended I wasn't there. "You were too busy on your fucking cell phone, dickhead." I was really pissed now. I didn't know where the rage came from, but it spewed out of me.

The asshole dad looked up at me, and frankly, at this point, I could care less what he was about to say. I just wanted to bash his face in. So I did. I didn't stop when the kid screamed, or when the poor dog barked. (Oddly, Ivan never bit or lunged at me). I just kept pounding at the guy's face, and loved it too. That's what scared me the most—how good it felt to feel his face getting slippery from snot and blood. And although my hand began to ache, I loved the sound of cracking bone when I hit hard. Only when another guy at the park ran up to pull me off did I let the dad go. I took one last look at him before walking away.

I knew then that I was losing it pretty bad, that my hold on sanity was loosening, but to be honest, I didn't give a shit.

FIFTH STITCH

On the drive to Wayne Manor, I thought about the phone call I'd had with Duffy a few days before, when I'd set up a time to meet. The strangest part of our short talk was that she hadn't once asked me about why I wanted to see her, nor did she express any worry over Trey. She just said, "Sure, come over any-time." When I mentioned I'd call first, she laughed and said, "Don't bother."

Heading toward Pasadena always reminded me of visiting my grandfather, who'd lived there until he'd died three years back. The city had a definite charm about it, with an old-money feel to its lush streets and countless neigh-borhoods with huge old houses behind hedges, gates, or perfect lawns. Most of my summers were spent swimming at the Valley Hunt Club pool, where I could order anything from the menu and write Granddad's number on the ticket instead of paying. It would be nice to see the city again, with the added bonus of visiting the iconic Wayne Manor.

The 210 had been flowing smoothly up until I got to Glendale, where a solid column of red taillights stopped my momentum. I took the time to check texts—none from Rache, and one from Trey, who did not know I was visiting his mom. It wasn't a good or comfortable feeling to go over my friend's head to get information from his mom, but there was no other way to find out more about Trish.

The biggest reason I felt impelled to go behind Trey's back and meet his mom was that I'd stopped trusting him. The visions were affecting my sense of who he was. He'd gone from a trusted friend to a potential cold-blooded killer, not someone likely to share the truth about his sister, especially if he'd killed her. Because Duffy was mother to both Trey and Trish, she might be willing to speak more openly.

Since traffic had stopped, I took the time to read Trey's text. He needed a favor, something about a soundcheck for his show. He asked if I could meet him at the gallery. I typed a quick "OK" and hit send. Trey had mentioned using Trish's poetry recordings as part of his soundtrack for the gallery opening. This could be my chance to hear Trish read her poetry without the dubbed-in music, the chattering guests, or any of the inevitable distractions that are part of gallery openings.

When I looked up, traffic had cleared and the cars ahead of mine now raced to make up for lost time. Disregarding the phone, I hit the accelerator with just as much eagerness as my fellow road mates. With an open road and speed on my side, I got to Suicide Bridge faster than I'd expected, and before I knew it I was on the exit Duffy had suggested.

Wayne Manor was awesome. It loomed on top of a huge, perfectly mani-cured grassy hill, just like the one I'd seen on TV. Bruce Wayne's enormous brick and stone mansion looked both ominous and stately from the street. I was growing more curious to see it up close.

The massive entry gates were closed when I drove up, but to my left and at driver's level was a call box. After pressing the red button, I heard the muffled sound of a ringing phone.

While the phone rang, I took to absentmindedly counting features on the house. There were ten chimneys, an octagonal turret, four stone balconies, and two wings on either side of the taller main structure. Based on the number of windows I counted, I figured there must be at least fifteen bedrooms in the place if not more. Then the phone stopped ringing, and a loud beep sounded just before the gates opened to let me in.

As I drove up the brick lane, I began to pick up a strange feeling from the place. It wasn't a bad feeling so much as a déjà vu sense of having been there before. Since it'd been used in tons of movies, as well as the *Batman* TV shows, I figured I recognized the house from those, so I dismissed the feel-ing as "film familiarity," a condition known to people in LA who see houses, buildings, or landmarks on film and later get a déjà vu sense when they see them in person.

At the top of the hill was a circular driveway that surrounded a massive fountain, and behind the fountain was the entry to the house. I parked on the side farthest from the house, got out, and approached the entry. The house loomed above me, casting late-afternoon shadows. Craning my neck to look at its highest point, it struck me that such a structure wouldn't be possible today. Wayne Manor was much taller than current building codes allowed—which gave it its unique monumental feel. Even the intricate brickwork and stone masonry on the façade was the handiwork of long-dead artisans; all of it was made during a time when such professions were valued.

The oversized, hand-carved front door was wide open, as if someone had been expecting me. I climbed the stone steps to the doorway and walked inside. The temperature was noticeably cooler inside the cavernous two-story entry hall, at the far end of which, directly facing me, was a wide flight of stairs that split apart at a second-story landing before separating toward opposite wings of the house. *Nice.*

"I still get lost, and I've lived here for over ten years." It was Duffy, the same woman from my first vision, now standing just four feet away from me. She was openly looking me over in an overly interested, almost sexual way that made me cringe. This present-day Duffy was older and fatter than the woman who'd been sucking off the black kid in my vision, but she was the same woman, without a doubt.

"Duffy, right?"

She grinned but not for long. Then she walked off and signaled for me to follow, so I did, walking behind her through double doors and into a large, wood-paneled room with a fireplace the size of my car. She plopped herself into one of four armchairs gathered in a square pattern around a large coffee table. The table, I soon noticed, was laid out with bongs, bags of weed, smaller bags filled with white powder, orange-tipped syringes, and more junk I didn't recognize.

I picked a chair and sat. What I hadn't noticed until I sat was that sitting in front of me was either a very old woman or a very old man dressed as a woman. He or she didn't seem to notice me even though I sat directly across from him or her.

"Aaron, say hi to Trcy's artist friend," Duffy addressed the old guy as she packed the bong with weed. Aaron brought a lace-gloved hand to his face, scratched at the corner of his eye, and nodded toward me but didn't say a word. He looked pretty stoned, so I didn't blame him for being quiet.

"Nice to meet you, Aaron." I tried to be friendly, but Aaron just stared at me. Weird dude, but somehow Aaron pulled it off with style. While trying not to stare back, it occurred to me Aaron was the first true eccentric I'd ever met. It also struck me how, without money or his big house, he'd be on the streets, and instead of being thought of as an eccentric he'd be a regular, crazy homeless guy.

Before I knew it, Duffy was inhaling deeply from a bong. It bubbled loudly, and suddenly Aaron began giggling and then laughing hysterically. He seemed oblivious to me watching him, as he went on about laughing at whatever inside joke had set him off. Duffy ignored him as she held her breath and passed the bong to me. Without thinking much about how being high might affect my visit, I took a hit and held it.

"You know me and Trey don't talk?" Duffy asked me while I held my breath, trying not to cough at the sharp smoke irritating my throat. So I nodded instead. "Is that why you wanted to see me?" Duffy fixed her eyes on me and waited for an answer. She glanced toward Aaron, who was still cackling but winding down with a sigh.

My throat burned and I forced back a cough while I exhaled. "One reason." I managed this before coughing pretty hard anyway. "I also wanted to know more about Trish."

Duffy nodded and looked down sadly at the mention of her daughter. Remaining quiet, she allowed me a few more hits, never flinching or commenting when I coughed. Then, without notice, Duffy took the lighter and the bong from me, set them back on the table, got up, and signaled for me to follow.

"Come, let me show you something," she said as she led me down a dark paneled hall and up a set of small stairs, at the top of which she stopped and opened a door.

"I thought you might like to see her work…Sometimes a person's art says more than they do. Don't you think?" Duffy asked as she stood at the doorway and addressed me.

I couldn't answer her or move. All I could do was stare past Duffy at the hallway behind her. It also struck me that I was suddenly feeling really high, *too high*. Even though I'd smoked only minutes ago, I was feeling the familiar surreal feeling from the pot.

But I was also scared shitless. Because behind Duffy all I could see was a shiny, long, white hallway. The very same white hallway I'd seen in the visions. The walls, the flooring, the lighting, all of it was the same as in the vision.

My heart pounded, and a panicky anxiety rushed through me, along with a strong urge to run. But I didn't run. I stood there staring, silently urging myself to calm down, and trying to convince myself that what I was looking at *couldn't be real*.

Even though I knew I was embarrassing myself, there was no way in hell I was going down that hallway, not again. Duffy stared at me quizzically. She whispered something that sounded like, "What did you say?" Or it might've been, "You okay?" but I couldn't be sure. She walked toward me until she was inches away, so close I smelled and felt her smoky breath on my face as she looked into my eyes.

"What? What is it?" she asked me, her tone urgent. But I kept my mouth shut. What could I say? That I'd seen her daughter tied up in a tub full of ice in a fucking vision right down this hall?

I wanted to answer, to suggest calmly that we go back the way we came, but I felt something up against my back. When I turned, the old guy—who I had no idea had followed us—was right in my face. He smiled, reached for my crotch, and squeezed my balls just before I shoved his gloved hand away, pushed him aside, and ran.

Unfortunately I went the wrong way. I must have. It all looked different. The floor changed from marble to wood, and the rooms were not the same rooms we'd passed on the way there. Sure, I was high on whatever shit Duffy had given me, but how hard can retracing your steps be? I ran back the way I thought we'd come but found myself in a smaller room, a type of office with a door at the end. I ran to it, opened it, and saw another, larger, empty room with a set of double doors at its end. The windows to this room led to the outside. There was a lawn visible beyond them, so I opened the window nearest me and climbed out, or rather fell out.

Hitting the ground feet first sent a pang up my calves, and without notice my knees buckled under me, so I stumbled to break my fall. The drop was much harder than I'd expected. When I glanced up at the open window, it looked like I'd jumped about ten feet. No wonder my ankle hurt. But I didn't stop; instead I hurried in the direction I hoped my car was.

It was getting dark, and I wanted to get the hell out of there, so I half hopped, half jogged to the other end of a stone wall too tall to climb over. I ran as fast as I could to the far end of it, hoping the circular driveway where I'd left my car would be on the other side. But when I turned the corner of the wall, I saw something else.

At first I couldn't believe what I was looking at. It was too improbable, too much to take in. During my short visit, things had added up. Things I had no way of knowing about had materialized before me. First I met Duffy, the same woman who'd been in my vision. Then I saw the white hallway—exactly like it had been in my vision. And now this. I suddenly regretted smoking the shit Duffy had given me. I wasn't sure if I was losing my grip on reality or just really high.

Either way, I stood before a live representation of my pen-and-ink drawing. It was perfect—an exact replica.

From where I stood, the lake and its surroundings were laid out in the same perspective as my drawing. There were the straggly trees at the far left end, the grasses, the San Gabriel Mountains above and behind it all, and lining the shore were the rocks. These, mercifully, did not have faces.

I fumbled inside my pocket, digging for my cell, hoping to get some pictures, anything to prove this small lake, this entire garden, had been real, but I'd left my phone in my car. So instead I stood and stared in fascination, studying every detail, hoping to find one flaw, one aspect that wasn't similar to my illustration, but I couldn't. I was about to leave when I heard footsteps behind me.

"Aaron will apologize later. He has a thing for young guys." Duffy was behind me; she must've come out through a side door and followed me. "We need to talk, you know."

I felt her hand on my shoulder and I fought an urge to shove her off. More than anything, I wanted Duffy's hand off me, and I wasn't sure why.

Even though I wanted to get the hell out of this place, I also wanted to hear what Duffy had to say. She'd mentioned Trish's artwork and I wanted to see it. What I hadn't expected was that Trish's work would lead to more questions than answers. So I stayed and walked back inside Wayne Manor with Duffy's hand on my shoulder.

"I caught them fucking." Those were Duffy's words. At first I was caught off guard by her bluntness, and then I realized I didn't know who or what she was talking about.

"What? You can't mean—"

"I caught Trey and Trisha fucking." She exaggerated her enunciation to be sure I understood.

I let this sink in. Trey and Trish hooked up? No way. They were...*related*. Why wouldn't Trey have said something? There was nothing I could think of to say. All I could do was wait for Duffy to say more, so I just sat there.

"I think it was a game for Trisha, but Trey was serious. He was totally into her."

We were back inside Wayne Manor, sitting in a huge room that served as a storage space. It was a big room too, up what was probably the north wing of the house. It looked like it could have been an attic once, but now it was cleanly drywalled, brightly lit with floods, and freshly painted to serve as place to keep extra furniture, clothes, and odds and ends.

My high was drifting off, which was a relief, since thinking clearly was becoming more and more important if I was to make sense of this weird-ass night. When I got home and had a chance to reflect, remembering things accurately would be a big help.

Duffy, though, kept taking hits from a joint she had with her. But besides her red-rimmed eyes, she never appeared stoned or in any way affected by the same weed that had unglued me. By the looks of her, and considering her history, I figured Duffy had developed a resistance to the stuff. We sat side by side on an old sofa, and I waited for Duffy to start talking. "Trey took it real hard when Trish disappeared. He took it harder when she left than when…" Duffy stopped and looked away. She was holding something back.

"When what?" I asked much too eagerly.

Her demeanor changed, from casual to sad to reflective. She was responding to something, something important, so I waited for her to either finish what she'd been about to say or rephrase it, but she held back. I stared at her profile until she turned to meet my gaze, hoping she'd go on and tell me more, but when she didn't, I couldn't help but prompt her again. "Trey took it harder than what? You were about to say more, Duffy."

She just stared back, no answer. I tried another angle. "So, it was incest, I mean, they were siblings…" Mentioning the obvious was a way to break her, or at least get an opinion out of her. Knowing what Duffy thought about her children having sex was suddenly important to me.

"They were *half brother and sister*," she corrected, "but I wasn't happy. I told both of them over and over they needed to cool off and stop. Trish promised, and Trey, well, he was in love."

It was there while sitting in the storage room with Duffy that I gave up any doubt that the girl I'd seen in my visions, the mangled girl on the basement floor, the girl in the tub, was Trish. All my previous attempts at doubt, all my hopes of exonerating my best friend of being a killer, dissolved in that bright room for good. Most people would likely think me slow to come to the conclusion, but you'll have to take into account that Trey had been my friend for a long time, and I thought I knew him. Besides, up until that point, the visions, however real they seemed, were still *visions*. There was one last way to find out for sure if Trish was the same girl I'd been seeing.

"Do you have any pictures of her? Of Trish?"

Duffy looked down when I asked this, then slowly and with great difficulty she hoisted her big body up enough to get off the couch. She waited to gather her balance before attempting to walk. Without looking back, she told me to wait.

Watching her walk out, I suddenly hoped that whatever picture she brought back would feature some girl who looked nothing like the one I'd come to know so well. The relief of anticipating a picture of a tall brunette, or a redhead, or any girl who looked totally different than the one in my visions, brought me a sense of hope.

With a pang of intense anxiety, the discomfort of coming down from a pot high began to take hold. Coming down from weed was one reason I'd stopped getting high as often as I used to. It was a shifty feeling of physical and emotional insecurity that overtook me as I waited for Duffy to come back. I changed my position on the couch and tried to shake off the growing depression. I was thinking about how good a beer would taste, when Duffy walked in holding an album under an arm and two bottles of Stella Artois gripped in her hand.

"Wow, you're a mind reader," I said as I took a bottle and the opener she held out. After quickly cracking open her cold beer, I opened mine and drank it down like it was water. Duffy sat down, managing to rock the old couch before setting the album down between us.

"Not really, but I do know beer takes the bite off a high. Anyway, here's Trish's album."

The lack of any affection in Duffy's tone escaped me, so eager was I to finally see pictures of Trish. After setting my bottle down on the floor next to me, I reminded myself not to rush or flip through the album too quickly once I held it.

Slowly turning the first page was difficult. There were no pictures on it, just girlish handwriting with overly curly words that were tough to read, but the carefully scribed "T&T" stuck out.

"I take it this stands for Trish and Trey?" I asked as I pointed. From the corner of my eye I saw Duffy nod.

It wasn't until the third page that I knew it was definitely her. On that page, there was a picture of Trish with the same blonde hair, the same green eyes, the same wide nose as the girl in the visions. My heart dropped as I studied picture after picture of a smiling, frolicking young kid who had no idea of the nightmare awaiting her.

Trey was in almost all the pictures. He, too, looked happy, unencumbered by whatever demon would later drive him to commit such a horrific act. If faces can reveal a dark soul under a human exterior, there was no sign of one on Trey's. His expressions revealed only a young kid, happy to be out with an older sister he openly worshiped.

Now that Duffy had revealed Trish and Trey's sexual affair, the pictures took on a different meaning. Moreover, now that I'd confirmed that the girl in the visions was Trish, the round belly I'd seen on her as she'd struggled in the tub suggested an additional, if not very different, motive.

Could Trish have been carrying Trey's baby? The thought began haunting me now more than ever.

I wondered if Duffy knew about Trish's pregnancy, but there was no way to ask without revealing my visions to her. As far as either Trey or Duffy knew, I'd never seen Trish or known she existed until recently.

Duffy tried to heave herself off the couch, but she plopped back down. She was a big woman; it took her another two tries, some rocking, and my help to hoist herself up. She walked to a stack of canvases that were covered by plastic sheeting and leaned neatly against the far wall. She began to pull them away from the wall as she talked.

"I sent most of Trish's stuff to Trey. He loved her work, and understood it. I certainly never did. But you have to give it to her, she was always creating, thinking, looking at things…Trish was always making stuff."

With my nearly finished beer in hand, I joined Duffy by the stacks. It occurred to me to mention Trey's plan to use Trish's poetry recordings at his show, but the sudden loud roar of a motor interrupted me. Whatever it was came from the other side of the open door we'd come through at the end of the massive room, but I couldn't see anything from where I stood.

But Duffy, seemingly less surprised than annoyed by the racket, began yelling, "Aaron! Aaron, stop!" at the top of her lungs, which only made things worse. She rushed toward the sound just as Aaron appeared at the doorway with a leaf blower strapped awkwardly onto his chest. He held the thing as best he could, pointing it at some invisible leaf pile, raising it up to blow Duffy in the face. She yelled and scolded him as she reached around him to grab at the machine in an apparent attempt to shut the thing off. She wasn't shy about roughing Aaron up either; she grabbed his shoulders and shifted his slight body around easily in her desperate hunt for a switch.

As Duffy frantically searched the contraption for a way to turn it off, Aaron kept aiming the mouth of the thing about like a crazy man. He aimed it at a piece of loose plastic sheeting, causing it to shoot up the wall and shiver against it. For some reason this brought Aaron great joy, and he laughed as he watched the plastic sheet flip and shake.

He'd changed clothes since I'd last seen him. He was now wearing a flowery, sleeveless dress with a wide but short hemline, and worn-out, plastic flip-flops. The cumbersome blower was loosely affixed to his narrow little body by thick straps that had caught onto his dress, pulling it up above his thighs at one point and well above his groin at another. I got an unwelcome but brief look at his huge red gonads and accompanying penis. I looked away, but not fast enough.

Duffy finally managed to switch the thing off, which caused Aaron to cry. It was a strange thing to see, an exhibitionist old guy in a dress crying like a kid. Fuck, I wanted to get out more than ever, but it was hard to look away from all the weird shit around me. Aaron dropped his head disconsolately and sobbed as Duffy struggled with the straps on the blower in an attempt to get the thing off him.

"You're supposed to strap it to your back…" Duffy huffed at Aaron, adding, "Oh dear."

She'd toned down and was being pretty gentle with the old guy, trying to comfort and sooth him. She patted his cheek and spoke to him in hushed tones. She either hadn't noticed or didn't care enough to pull Aaron's dress down over his shriveled dick. But when she realized her soothing tone wasn't working, she raised her voice and threatened, "Oh, stop crying, or I won't play with the Captain," Duffy said in a singsong, childish sort of way, which was fucked up, because the next thing she did was grab his cock.

That was when I made a more aggressive move to leave, but Duffy stopped me. "Don't go! Not yet!" The only thing that kept me there was the promise of seeing Trish's artwork, so I stood in place, not wanting to risk sitting back down and prolonging the visit.

"Listen, Duffy…I've got stuff to do," I said, walking toward her only because she stood near the door.

Aaron finally let Duffy unstrap the blower from his torso, allowing his dress to drop back below his knobby knees. Without a glance at either of us, he dejectedly made his way over to the old couch.

"He loves that thing." Duffy turned toward me and laughed. "Before you go, you must see what's left of Trish's paintings." She rushed back to the large rectangular canvas she'd been uncovering when Aaron interrupted, pulled it out from the rest, and held it up for me to see.

It's hard to explain what I noticed first or where my gaze initially landed on the canvas. So much can happen in a split second. What I remember was feeling choked when I took in the painting Duffy held; it was like I'd forgotten how to breathe.

The canvas was starkly organized and featured three toy dolls lined up across its width. The dolls were the plastic, flesh-colored ones sold everywhere, the ones that looked like chubby babies. The three babies sat in a row from left to right, and all were naked. My eyes dropped to their genitals, where thick black stitches appeared, although it was hard to tell if these were male or female dolls. I didn't need to look long to notice the mouths of all three were also crudely sewn shut.

My expression must have given away my confusion and shock, because Duffy felt compelled to explain. "Trish used real dolls as models. She'd sew them up with black yarn. Weird, I know. I asked her what it meant. All I remember was something about it being a misogynistic ritual, an ancient way of demeaning women."

Duffy uncovered more of the paintings, and after my initial shock I began to understand the theme Trish had been after. The work was pretty disturbing in its own right, but add the visions I'd been having, and I was ready to get the hell out.

By now there was no way in hell I was hanging around any longer, but before I could stop myself, I said, maybe a little too loudly, "Okay, that's enough, really. I'm, ah...listen, it's nice of you to show me all of her work, but I need to head back."

Duffy nodded and turned back to rifle through the stack until she found a small canvas wrapped in paper. She held it out and handed it to me. "Here, you'll need this."

"I can't take her painting...What, what do you mean I'll need it?"

Aaron smiled at me from the couch as he watched. Something about Duffy's stubborn expression told me she wasn't going to let me go unless I accepted her gift, so I took the painting. At this point in the evening, I was less curious about the painting than driven to get out and head home. So I said my good-byes, thanked Duffy, and left with one of Trish's paintings under my arm.

It wasn't until I'd driven out of Pasadena that I pulled the car over to the curb. The urge to see the painting suddenly overtook me, so after I stopped and clicked on the overhead light, I grabbed it, ripping away the paper and bubble wrap in a few quick rips to uncover it.

In the dim yellowish light of the car, the two plastic baby dolls appeared to jump out of the canvas. They were the same type of baby dolls I'd seen in her other work, but these were different. These babies weren't flesh colored; these were painted a solid, sickly grey, giving them a cadaver-like appearance. Both had the same grotesque, thick black stitching on their mouths and genitals. But my eyes were drawn to the distinctly grey skin of the two, made all the more sickly by the light orange color Trish had selected for the background.

After I clicked off the overhead light, I sat back and remembered Trey's annoying chant: "Grey is dull." I remembered how I'd heard it during the vision only to come out of it to hear the real Trey chanting it too. He'd said his show was about blacks and whites mixing, and how when they did they made grey. And here I had a painting where Trish—who I was sure had been pregnant at the time she'd been tortured and killed—had painted two grey babies. Was this her way of expressing or representing biracial issues? Perhaps even babies resulting from a union with her half brother?

There was no way to find out now unless I asked Trey or maybe even Duffy, but there was little chance I'd do that. After restarting the car, waiting for traffic to clear, and pulling out onto the street, the strangeness of the catch-22 circumstance I was in struck me. The painting Duffy had given me had only produced more questions. But who could I speak to? Who could I turn to with all my questions without revealing the visions?

After driving for a mile or two in hilly and winding residential streets that grew darker and more thickly treed, I was suddenly and violently slammed from behind without warning. Weirder still, I hadn't seen lights or noticed another car behind me.

It was a hard and shocking blow—the sort of collision you see when a car accelerates toward its target with no intention of stopping. The inertia of the impact whipped me in the direction of my steering wheel like a giant hand slapping the back of my head. In slow motion I saw the steering wheel rushing toward me, but I was powerless to stop it—until the magnificent white explosion of the air bag interceded. The white of the bag turned to black in a flash when I lost consciousness.

SIXTH STITCH

"YOU WENT TO SEE MY MOM?" Trey's pissed voice echoed at me from the blackness.

Where was I? Why the echo? A light was switched on and the blackness turned into an achingly bright white light. My first reaction was to close my eyes against the brightness, but as I slowly opened them to a squint, I saw only white tile surrounding me.

I was back in the bathroom, the one in Duffy's house. Trey was off to my right and sitting on the edge of the white tub, just like I'd seen him in the last vision. *Oh fuck! Was I in a vision?*

As my eyes grew more accustomed to the brightness, I saw he was holding a long, sharp needle threaded with thick, black yarn.

"What do you want with Duffy anyway? A blow job?" Trey's eyes met mine with determination. He looked right at me as if it was perfectly normal to be with him in a bathroom while he held a thick, threaded needle.

I tried to speak, but no words came out. Trey shook his head like he was disappointed and turned toward the tub. As soon as he did, the tinkling sound of the ice-filled water became more frenetic and was followed by splashing. My heart began to beat wildly, because I knew Trish had to be in the tub.

Just like before, I closed my eyes, but there was no darkness, no relief, just the white bathroom and Trey. Closing my eyes to block a visually disturbing image wasn't an option. As hard as I clamped my lids shut, I still *saw*. The vision remained. My inability to not see made the visions all the harder to endure.

"How fucked is that? You and Duffy hanging out?" Trey chuckled his disgust, but his real attention was on Trish inside the tub. His expression changed when he looked down at her. His disgust softened into a contorted smile—a smile more patronizing than loving.

While he bent over the tub with the threaded needle in his hand, I tried to move, to shift my body on the floor where I was sprawled, but I couldn't. The splashing from the tub became frantic, and over the edge I could see part of Trish's knees. They were bound together with duct tape. She struggled while Trey's fingers pinched and pulled her upper lip away from her face. The rags Trey had stuffed inside her mouth to prevent her from yelling or calling out were so bloodied, it was impossible to tell what their original color had been.

"We've got to get you ready, girl." Trey's tone was kind and patient as he looked down on Trish.

All I could do was watch as he passed the needle through the first open hole on the farthest right corner of her top lip. From where I sat against the cold tile wall, I could see Trish's face. I saw her bloody teeth and lips and tried to make eye contact with her, hoping that by doing so I could offer her hope or the strength to endure the pain, but even though Trish's eyes were wide open, almost gaping, they were focused upward at the ceiling.

Maybe looking up and away was how she withstood what must have been the terrible sensation of yarn being drawn through a hole in her lip. Maybe by looking up at the ceiling, Trish could remove herself from this bathroom and Trey's cruelty and imagine herself elsewhere.

Trey pulled at the yarn and I noticed a bump under Trish's lip. That bump must have been the knot that kept the yarn from slipping through. After tugging it tautly, he took his free hand and pulled out Trish's lip, this time the lower one.

Trish's body suddenly began shaking violently, splashing bloody water over the tile around her. There were blood splatters on the wall and smears on the tub where she'd rubbed her cheek. It looked like she was having some sort of fit, because she shook and splashed until Trey roughly grabbed her by the hair and pressed her head against the porcelain tub. Trish stopped moving. She laid her head back and closed her eyes.

"You know, after we're done here, I'm fixing you so you can keep your babies. You wanna keep your babies, don't you?"

Trish knew exactly what this meant, because she'd reopened her eyes and looked right at me. This time when our eyes met I knew she could see me, and I finally sensed she realized I meant no harm. As I stared into her eyes, an intense feeling of helplessness overcame me, but with no way of communicating my desire to help her, my helplessness felt vast and intolerable.

Then Trey said the one thing that convinced me everything I knew and had witnessed was true: "Come on now. No one but you wants grey babies. What good are mixed, muddied, soiled, grey babies? Huh?" Trey smirked and laughed.

A rush of will suddenly built up in me. Maybe it was driven by rage, or maybe I was getting better at controlling my actions during a vision. Either way, it felt like finding an elusive itch or catching a fly in midair—tough, but not impossible. Somehow I dredged up resolve and managed to scream. It wasn't easy, and it came out sounding like a howl, but I managed to grunt out, "Tre...sssstop!"

Trey stopped what he was doing, the bloody needle frozen in midstitch as he slowly turned to glance at me before casually resuming his work.

Then a searing pain in my back woke me. I sat up on my couch, which made the sharp pain shoot up my neck. My clothes were drenched in sweat, and I was shaking pretty hard, but the more I looked around and saw my things, my walls, and knew I was back in my own apartment, the calmer I got.

I lay back and tried piecing together the time I'd lost. Then it came back to me—the car accident after leaving Duffy's, the seatbelt pulling me away from the steering wheel right before the air bag inflated in my face.

The recollection of blacking out at the wheel came back. Somehow, after all of it, I'd driven myself to a local emergency room. They'd asked if the other guy, the guy who'd rear-ended me, had stopped. Lying had been surprisingly easy, I recalled, because without hesitation I'd told the nurse he'd split, left the scene. I shamelessly claimed I'd been the victim of a hit and run.

The lie had come out so easily because there was a shitload to cover up. Not only had I still been high, but as soon as I'd regained consciousness and woke up in the dark, a wild rage had overtaken me. After I was able to focus and saw the draped fabric of the airless airbag on my lap, saw the shiny shards of glass from my shattered back windshield, all I wanted, the only thing on my mind, was to fight. At that point it could have been a woman and I'm pretty sure I would have done the same thing—beat the crap out of her. But I suppose I was lucky to have been hit by a guy, because I'd never hit a girl before, and living with that would have been fucking hard. Maybe I was falling to pieces under the strain of these fucked-up visions and needed to vent, or maybe I was still under the effect of Duffy's weed, but as I sat surrounded by pieces of my windshield, the only thing that felt right was violence.

Poor guy didn't know what hit him. He'd done the right thing and come over to see how I was. The picture of him standing by my window and looking into my car was still clear in my mind. But the only thing I thought to do when I'd seen him was swing my door open and slam him.

When I got out of the car and joined him on the deserted street, he was bowled over with the air knocked out of him. Somehow, in that moment, it occurred to me to walk over and check the back of my car. The damage seemed small compared to the force of the impact, but that didn't stop me from heading over to the guy for more.

The fact that he was bent over somehow pissed me off, so I grabbed him by the shoulder, whipped him around, and punched him on the jaw. My fist slipped off his cheek, and a sharp sting rose up my arm. When I reached back to swing again, his face seemed frozen in place, like he was waiting for my fist to slam him again. In the dim light, I watched as his straight, black hair flew back from the force of my second punch. His hands came up to his face as if to protect it, or maybe I'd broken his nose. No way to tell in the dark. I could see he was a few years older than me, with dark skin, so I figured he was either Middle Eastern or Mexican.

When he raised his head and opened his mouth to speak, I struck again, and again, so many times that any play-by-play description of the beating would be impossible.

I heard him say something, or try to, which only made me hate this dude (who, by the looks of the Staple's logo on his red T-shirt and the pinned-on plastic tag claiming his name was Steve, was probably a hard-working guy) enough to continue to kick his ass.

I don't know why I kicked Steve's ass. I do remember thinking about Trey the whole time. I guess deep down I wished it had been Trey I'd been beating.

When I felt less groggy, I managed to get up and sit on the edge of the couch. Pain meds—I'd need more soon. For now I was mostly numb, but waiting too long would allow the pain to rekindle. The memory of the intense throb in my hand, now neatly bandaged, and the ache in my back (which would only get worse if I didn't take something) was enough to get me up.

I stood by the couch to let the dizziness subside, and then I saw something dark and bundled on my rug. I froze in place and stared at it. I even blinked, hoping it would go away. But it didn't. It was a ball of black yarn, the loose end leading down the narrow hall before it turned into my bathroom.

I walked slowly toward the bathroom to follow it but hesitated before looking in. If this was going to be another vision, I wanted to be ready for it. My fight-or-flight instinct hollered for me to run, but I was too weak.

I flicked on the bathroom light, and there, on the floor, propped against the sink, was the painting Duffy had given me. Trish's painting of the two grey babies. The bathroom light made the babies seem more grotesque; their sewn mouths appeared to be grinning, their sewn genitals just plane cruel. I bent down to pick up the black yarn, but it was gone. I could have sworn on my father's grave it had been there. The yarn had been real, but now it was gone, just like that.

The phone rang in the other room, but I stood still. All I could do was stare at the grey babies against the orange background. I suddenly understood what Trey had meant about the color grey. Grey *was* dull, and in a very disturbing way, grey was beginning to look like death to me.

On the counter above the painting was the bottle with pain meds the hospital had sent me home with. With the phone still ringing in the living room, I popped a Vicodin and stuck my head under the faucet to wash it down.

My antiquated but handy answering machine picked up the call, and Trey's voice came on. From where I stood, it was impossible to tell what he was saying. All I could hear was his steady tone—so different from the creepy one in the vision.

I stared at the grey babies, wondering how maybe Trey might have felt less loved or wanted because of his mixed race. Not really white and not really black. His black relatives would have noticed his lighter skin, while his white relatives would have noticed the darker. All his life, he must have picked up on those nuances. How could he not? It must have been hard for him to watch as Trish got more attention while growing up. Falling for her later would definitely have confused the crap out of him. But still, mutilation, torture, and murder?

I walked back toward the couch and heard the last part of his message.

"…coming to the soundcheck or not? Don't forget the opening is next week. I'm counting on you to be there, bro. I even invited these crazy chicks I met at a club last night. Don't bail on me, dude."

Fuck, I'd not gotten back to him about the soundcheck. I'd call him when I felt better. For now, all I could do was hobble back to the couch for more sleep.

The phone rang again. All I could do was curse it; I was too groggy to think about answering it. But what if it was Rache finally getting back to me? I managed to raise my head, but as soon as I did, everything changed.

That's how fast they came on lately. I could swear the visions were timed to start in the split second I blinked. Gone were the shaky visual effects of the first hallucination, where pixels appeared. Gone was any helpful sense of transition. No, this time it was just—*bam*, there I was.

I was back on the lush grounds at Wayne Manor in Pasadena. I stood on a large lawn with Aaron, standing about four feet away from me, smoking the biggest joint I'd ever seen.

He wore a multi-color miniskirt, some sort of hippy- chick platform shoes, and a greasy, loose-fitting, wife-beater undershirt. The reason I know it was a mini-skirt was that his old-man cock was visible at the hemline, *again*. I was beginning to realize just how much of an exhibitionist Aaron was.

Aaron smiled and held out the joint for me. That was when I realized this vision was different. I was able to move, to shake my head no. He shrugged his shoulders and took another drag from his spliff while I struggled to put words together. If I could speak, this would be my big chance to ask Aaron major questions about Trish. Maybe he knew about her relationship with Trey or if anyone had known she'd been pregnant.

But trying to speak was hard. The harder I focused on it, the more it felt like my tongue was either numb or being held down. I mustered all my strength to make a sound, to break the uncomfortable barrier, that awful feeling of muscle paralysis. My first attempt produced a muttering sound. Then finally I broke through and stammered, "Didddd?" This time it felt a little easier, so I kept trying. "Di-di-did...kill he-he-her?"

I stared at Aaron, waiting for a sign of comprehension, but all he did was stare back at me absentmindedly while grabbing at his shriveled dick. A pretty pathetic picture it made, too. There I was, trying to verbalize and ask vital questions of a wasted and most likely insane old man who seemed more amused by me than concerned.

But it was all I had, so I tried again. "Whaa twa-twa-twins? *Lisssssten.*"

Then I heard Duffy, and we both turned to watch her running toward us from about fifty feet away. Aaron suddenly became all business. He let go of his cock, stuck the joint between his teeth, and ran, but not very fast, not in those shoes.

I jogged alongside him through parts of the garden I'd not seen, curious to know where he was going. When we got to a brick and stone Tudor cottage, he stopped. The cottage was a smaller version of the mansion, most likely a former guest or caretaker house. Using the hand that held the big joint, Aaron pointed at the building and said, "In there."

"Baaaabies?" The cottage looked deserted, the windows were boarded shut, and the door had a padlock on the outside. I walked to the cottage and realized the uselessness of it all; the place looked completely uninhabitable, no light could come in, no air, nothing.

Aaron sucked away at his joint, before shaking his head and mumbling, "Big trouble."

"Aaron!" Duffy screamed. She ran up to us, red faced and totally out of breath. She was pissed, too. She violently grabbed Aaron by the arm and began to spank him on the ass like a child, but harder. He smiled, and I couldn't help but notice that his fucking skirt was hitched up again. The old guy was liking it.

"O-o-o-open!" I commanded Duffy while pointing to the cottage, but she, unlike Aaron, couldn't hear or see me.

"You are *not* to go near the cottage, Aaron! You have to promise you won't tell anyone about it."

I heard her slap the old guy's ass. Aaron looked at me and grinned a sinister smile. The last thing I noticed before the vision ended was that Aaron finally got the boner he'd wanted all along.

Just as quickly as I'd left my apartment, I was back in it. The rage came back then, and something inside me, something hard to describe, a seething inner jolt of anger shot through my body. It was stronger than ever, and I did my best to quell it. I had to learn to control this rage. I had to, or I would end up killing someone. A distraction. I needed a distraction.

What I really needed was to talk to someone, but so far, the only person I'd confided in was Rachel, and she hadn't responded to any of my texts. It was pissing me off. Even if she was dating someone, wouldn't she text back and just say so? Could this new guy be so insecure he'd flip out if she returned one of my calls?

After finding my phone in the living room, I scrolled down to Rachel's number. After the fourth ring, her voice mail picked up, and I struggled to think of what to say.

"Hey, it's me. Just wondering what's up, why you won't call me back. Listen, I've texted you like eight times, so I figure you're probably seeing someone, but, fuck, Rache...I need to talk to you." The rage began to surge and I aimed my anger at her. "Fuck whoever this guy is. The visions are worse, Rache. You're the only one who knows." Raising my voice and gritting my teeth now, I went on. "You're the only one I can talk to. You have insight. How did you know about the pink phone? *Did I even tell you about the pink phone?* You have to help me!"

I threw the phone against the wall, which started a wild-ass rage I couldn't control. One hard kick to my coffee table sent it and all the crap on it flying. With one swing of my arm, a stack of books, bills, and magazines flew off the kitchen counter. The crusted plate that still had some of last night's uneaten dinner on it smashed against the wall behind my sofa.

A loud thumping on the floor came from Stan's place downstairs. I yelled at the top of my lungs to be sure he could hear me. "Fuck you, Stan! I never fucking make noise!" Then I swiped the iPod receiver off the console and slammed it against the wall.

As the rage took over, the thought of heading downstairs and getting into it with Stan seemed appealing, but it wouldn't be enough. It would only make me feel as helpless as I had after beating up the guy at the park and the poor dickhead who rear-ended me. As good as this felt, there was something missing. What was missing was Trey. He was the real source of my rage.

Seeing the vivid image of Trey's smile as he taunted a bound and gagged Trish, I began to automatically search through my drawers. I opened them and let all the contents spill out onto the floor. Without thinking, it hit me that I was looking for something. While some inexplicable inner voice directed me, I began to look for a tool—something thin, long, and metal.

The mistake I'd made all along was that I'd been aiming my rage at the wrong people. It was Trey who deserved the retribution, not random assholes who had offended me.

Lately I'd been entertaining a fantasy in which I hurt Trey and inflicted the same fear and pain he'd so savagely caused Trish. Some fantasies had a way of remaining just that, fantasies, unlikely to seep into reality. But the ones I was having about Trey were growing into pretty strong urges—not mild urges like cravings, but a deep-down, innate need to hurt him.

Oddly, when I'd had the fantasies about hurting Trey, they didn't feel bad or even wrong. No, these urges, when they came, felt good, pure, and right, just like being in love felt right. And just like love, there was a time and a place to act.

Sometimes, I told myself, the things you wanted in life lined up for you, and other times you had to line them up yourself. This was one of those times when I needed to do the lining up.

I stopped my rampage and stood panting in my living room, allowing the calmness to come over me. With the sudden clarity of knowing I needed to target Trey and no one else, I was able to calm down. I'd been a victim to random spats of violence that served no purpose other than hurting the wrong people. Suddenly, that night, I realized I had a distinct purpose.

———————————————

Trey had asked me to meet him at the gallery and give him feedback on the soundtrack for the opening. It was my chance to finally hear Trish's voice reading her poetry, so there was little chance I'd miss that. In fact, I found myself savoring the moment.

I worked off steam by walking to the gallery. Besides, I didn't want Trey noticing the damage to the back of my car and ask questions.

About a block away, I could hear loud, rhythmic pounding coming from inside the industrial building housing the prestigious and impossible to get into CWG gallery. The closer I got, the clearer the sounds became, until the continuous electronic percussion no longer overpowered the voice of the girl—*Trish*. That was her voice. I stopped walking and listened, not really hearing what she was saying, but taking in the sound of *her*.

I stood in the dark for some time just listening before I knocked on the side door of the gallery. Seconds later, Trey stuck his head out and gestured for me to come in.

"Hey, bro, thanks for coming, I was wondering if you'd make it. You know how it is...I'm starting to question everything I do."

He looked down at my still-bruised, swollen, and cut hand, which I'd forgotten about. "Whoa, what happened?"

"Ah, you don't want to know. It's not a big deal." Looking at my own messed-up hand to avoid eye contact with Trey was a convenient way to drop the subject while appearing embarrassed. I craned my neck to look behind him and asked, "Are you gonna let me in?"

Trey broke a smile and began walking down a short hallway. I followed him into the messy back offices of the gallery, where canvases and empty frames leaned against the walls. By the looks of it, this was utilitarian space, the place where the business of selling art was done, where windows weren't needed, and where appearances didn't matter. The two retro metal desks piled high with paperwork and takeout containers were even more evidence of it being a place for work.

It was the soundtrack that played on overhead speakers that attracted most of my attention. I was trying hard to listen, but Trey kept staring at my hand, which did look pretty bad in the office lighting. "Fuck, dude, your hand..." Then he got all concerned and said, "You draw with that hand."

As soon as he said it, it dawned on me that, hell, he was right. But why hadn't I thought of it first? Was I losing it that badly? Trey was right. I would have to call Tina and finagle more time on the last six drawings. The feeling of not being in total control of my life suddenly hit me. I'd have to deal with that later.

In response to Trey's comment, all I could say was, "I'll deal with it."

There was an uncomfortable silence while he continued to stare at me, as if waiting for me to say more. But I didn't. All I wanted, the only reason I'd come, was to listen to the soundtrack.

"If you're in some kind of trouble, you should say something, man." Trey finally looked away from my hand and asked, "Is it something with Rache?"

He was talking too much, talking over Trish's voice, and it was aggravating. I didn't want to answer his question. It wasn't any of his business what I was going through—not anymore. In between Trey and the annoying electronic percussion mixed on the soundtrack, I heard snippets of Trish's young, all-too-serious, but determined voice sounding stiff as she read her poetry.

Trey finally changed the subject from me to his show. "Yeah, well, this show's got me going crazy. It's not that I'm ungrateful or shit like that, it's—"

I didn't have patience for his shit, so I broke right in. "That's Trish now, isn't it?"

Trey nodded and looked at me weird. He sat down on a rolling Eames chair and kicked the matching one toward me. With my unhurt hand, I stopped the chair from rolling or making unnecessary noise so I wouldn't miss a word of the tinny recording of Trish reading her poetry.

it's the best I can hide with no walls,

it's the hardest I can push with no will,

this is the fastest I can run with what I have

My heart began to race, but this time I wasn't feeling fear but sheer hatred. Just being in the same room with Trey was a struggle. This poem, these words had so much meaning for me. How could Trey not react to them?

"What did she mean by 'the fastest I can run'?" I asked, waiting for Trey to show interest, but he didn't. He was reading his texts and didn't look up when he answered.

"How should I know? She was a kid when she wrote it."

That was his best answer? "How old was she when wrote this?"

It was really hard for me to look Trey in the eye now, knowing what I knew. To be totally honest, I wanted to bash his face in, but I kept my cool.

"Seventeen, maybe sixteen, I think. What do you think about the static?" He looked up from his fucking phone now. "My buddy says it gives it texture. Is it too distracting?"

Fuckhead didn't care about what she was saying. He only cared how good it would sound at his opening.

Still, I held it together. "Keep the static. Without it her voice would be too present, too real, too in your face." What I meant to say, what I should've said, was, "Without the static, she would sound too *alive*. She's gone. You killed her, so why make it sound like she isn't dead?" But I didn't. There was time for that later.

"Good point. Soundtrack's insane, isn't it?" Trey was reaching out to me, I could tell. He knew something was up. Not only did he look uncomfortable, but I could see it in the way he looked at me, keeping his eyes on me too long as if searching for clues, or hoping I'd chill. I knew he wasn't the type to bring it up and say, "Hey, dude, what's wrong with you?" No, Trey let problems ride—until they went away.

"So, show me the space. I haven't seen anything from your series yet." I said this while walking over to what looked like an entry to the main gallery. Trey had been pretty secretive with his new series and hadn't posted any pictures of it on his website. It was unlike him, but then it could have been a stipulation from CW Gallery that he not show pictures of his work on his website. Some galleries liked having the chance for a first show of an artist's work, even refusing to post pictures on their own websites.

Trey leaned over and flipped off the tape. Trish's voice stopped cold—right at the word *grey*. Of all the words the recording could've stopped at, it stopped at the most significant one I could think of. Like some psychic message, or nod of encouragement urging me to go ahead with retribution and revenge, the tape had been stopped at *grey*.

When he stood up, he shook his head and laughed as if to lighten the mood. "No way. No one gets to see anything until the opening. Besides, it's not all hung yet. Come on, let's get out of here. I'm getting sick of this place. You wanna get a beer...on me?"

I declined his invitation quickly and maybe too harshly. It was easy now that no doubt remained that he'd killed his sister, something only a true sociopath could pull off.

That Trey was a sociopath was becoming glaringly evident. When I'd googled it—out of sheer curiosity—I'd found hundreds of sites, most of which offered lists of traits typically found in sociopaths. The lists were extremely helpful. All uncannily described Trey and were instrumental in explaining how he could appear normal and well adjusted to the rest of society while being capable of a sick and gruesome crime. The personality traits included:

- Glibness and superficial charm
- Manipulative and cunning
- Pathological lying
- Lack of remorse
- Inability to love but adept at mimicking or going through the motions
- Need for stimulation tending toward the artistic
- Lack of empathy

With the knowledge that my friend Trey was a skilled impostor, with all the evidence pointing toward his affinity for cruelty, I had no qualms about treating him with disdain. After I'd made my excuses so brusquely, it was pretty easy to ignore his hurt expression and leave.

What Trey didn't know was that all I could think of was getting to Balk's Hardware before they closed so I could get on with my plan.

SEVENTH STITCH

WALKING AS FAST AS I COULD, heading east on Melrose, the idiom about giving someone a taste of his own medicine, a saying I'd once thought offensive, was all I could think of. Giving Trey a taste of his own medicine was beginning to take on new meaning. It used to be I believed most, if not all, people were capable of empathy. For those incapable of showing concern for others, I trusted karma to carry out whatever payback it saw fit to serve. But what about people like Trey, who tortured and killed and went about their lives unscathed? In other words, how else would a sociopath know what it felt like to be tied down and tormented?

The further east I walked on Melrose, the grittier and less uptown the shops and restaurants got. Here the sex shops boldly displayed all kinds of sex toys and dominatrix paraphernalia in their windows, the tattoo parlors featured cheaper neon signs, the number of auto mechanic shops increased. On this part of Melrose, you could bet the stores were run by struggling private owners as opposed to franchises, like those on the ritzy western section of the avenue.

Since the gentrification of Melrose, the true hardcore punk shops that had gained the district so much fame in the '80s and '90s had been forced out by increasing rents and higher-income clientele. Here, in the low-scale district, was where Flaco the drug dealer kept his business. Flaco was a short, overweight, small-time dealer who'd survived in the dwindling Melrose drug trade by his stubborn refusal to move further east or south. Like I knew he would be, Flaco was lingering inside Martha's Mom, a medicinal marijuana store where he'd set up shop after the more favorable pot laws passed.

When I walked into Martha's, Flaco called out a welcome in his typical LA Mexican singsong. "You been away, haven't you? I was at Barney's the other night and didn't see you, man."

"Yeah, well, I've been workin' a lot. Listen, Flaco, I've got like eighty bucks. Set me up with some weed, something strong, dude."

Flaco smirked and got up off his stool without another word. Although I was in a hurry, telling Flaco so would only slow him down; the guy had a knack for testing your patience. After what seemed like forever, he reappeared from the back holding a small package wrapped in white paper.

"You got your hall pass, amigo?" Flaco was referring to the semibogus medical marijuana cards required to legally buy pot. I couldn't help but chuckle when I pulled it out of my wallet and held it out so Flaco could jot down the numbers.

"Such government bullshit," Flaco mumbled under his breath as he wrote. I pulled out the eighty bucks and dropped it on the glass counter before grabbing the white package and hurrying back out onto the sidewalk. My "later dude" was returned with Flaco's sarcastic, "Wham, bam, thank you, ma'am."

About four blocks from Flaco's, I heard footsteps behind me. Usually I wouldn't have paid much attention, but since I'd just bought weed, I was feeling paranoid. When I turned around to look, all I saw was a slight woman in the shadows, and so I relaxed and didn't give it any more thought.

By the time I got to Balk's, it looked like they were near closing time. The lights inside were dimmer than usual, and the stand-alone signs they kept on the sidewalk advertising all kinds of shit had been taken inside.

Balk's was a one-stop, old-time, mom-and-pop-type hardware store packed with most everything you could need. The old guys who ran it were really thorough about stocking all kinds of crap. They were pretty cool too. They kept a big bowl of popcorn on the counter next to the store's official cat, a cat aptly named Mechanic. Mechanic was a big orange and white tabby so used to being petted by strangers that she didn't get up when touched. Instead she kept her eyes closed, laid still, and purred.

"You have ten minutes before closing," one of the old guys called out from the back.

"Where do you guys keep ice picks?" I felt weird calling this out, especially while enjoying the typical eighty-degree, subtropical LA weather, but hell.

"Ice picks? Let's see...Go to the bolt bin, look above that, and you'll see one, maybe two."

The bolt bin was near the window, toward the end of the store; I'd noticed it the last time I'd been in. I rushed toward the big green sign hanging from the ceiling that read, "Nuts, screws, and bolts." I found the ice picks right away. They were hard to miss, since they were the only things gleaming in the dull lighting.

Taking the ice pick from the hook where it hung, I made my way back to the center of the store. I heard the cluster of bells on the front door rattle, but outside of wondering if the old guy was going to kick the late customer out, I took little notice.

The duct tape was up front. That I knew, because I'd seen a bucketful near the counter when I'd walked in. When I got to the register, there was a woman there, most likely the latecomer, waiting for one of the old guys to come out. I stood behind her thinking she looked similar to the lady I'd seen walking behind me earlier, but she kept her back to me while she petted Mechanic.

"Hey, man, you got customers out here," I yelled out for the old guy.

Finally he walked out from the back, looked at me, then at the ice pick and said, "Ah, good, you found it."

I felt bad because he was totally ignoring the lady who was not only first in line but facing him at the counter. So I said, "She was here first."

The attendant looked at me really weird. "Who you mean?"

The next thing I remember was how the woman stopped petting the cat and turned to look at me. It was then that I realized it was Aaron, that it had been him all long, and that he'd followed me here.

"Aaron," I said. "Why the fuck are you following me?"

He was wearing a much more conservative dress, no miniskirt this time. He glanced knowingly at the ice pick and duct tape I held. He looked at them with such recognition that I could tell immediately he knew why I had them and what I planned to do with them.

"Hey, are you on something?" The old guy behind the counter asked me. "You need help?"

It was then that I realized he couldn't see Aaron. I must have looked pretty weird to him, standing there getting pissed at no one. The poor guy looked concerned, maybe even worried for me. "You feeling okay?"

"Aaron, speak up, or get the fuck out of my way," I said, getting right in Aaron's face.

The poor old guy behind the counter just stared at me. Out of the corner of my eye, I saw him grab the phone, which is what I would've done, but it didn't faze me. If he was calling the police, I had time to find out why Aaron had followed me well before any cop got here.

With his eerie blue eyes focused on mine, Aaron finally nodded toward the ice pick and tape and said, "You don't know enough for that. You're going too far." He put a hand on my shoulder and gave me a sad look before walking away.

All I could do was stand there and stare at the sleeping cat curled up on the counter, wishing more than anything for that kind of total peace. But there was no chance of it, not for me. The familiar thumping in my chest returned, along with the dreaded anxiety that came with my visions.

By now the old guy was frantically talking to a dispatcher on the phone, trying to clarify whether a cop or a paramedic should be sent out. With wary eyes, he watched me as he did a play-by-play of my movements for the dispatcher. "He's just standing there now not moving...no, I don't think he's drunk...it could be he's taken something."

I turned to leave and heard him go on, "He's turning. Looks like he's leaving now. If you guys are gonna help, you better get here soon."

At the door it occurred to me that I should probably hurry to avoid any trouble with the police, since I did have a good amount of weed on me. I shot out of Balk's and ran as fast as I could. It wasn't until I was a block from my apartment that I stopped and noticed I'd taken and not paid for the tape and the ice pick.

A few days later, I got around to working out my plan. Being organized was important if I was going to do this right. It wasn't a difficult thing to figure out, the plan sort of wrote itself. The one thing I knew was essential was that it had to take part on the night of Trey's opening.

My Ten-Part Plan:

1. Invite Trey to stay at my place after his opening. (This was probably what he was planning to do anyway, since he usually stayed at my place after he hit clubs in town.)

2. Fill my tub halfway with water before going to his show. Add the bags of ice just before Trey got here.

3. Get Trey wasted on Flaco's weed and vodka.

4. When the moment was right, when he's both stoned and drunk, surprise him and hold him down, then bind his legs and arms with duct tape. (Since I had an easy sixty pounds and almost a foot in height on him, this wouldn't be a problem. Besides, when Trey got wasted enough, he didn't much care or know what the hell was going on.)

5. Stuff his mouth with rags and drag him into the bathroom. (Keeping the noise level down was key. Stan downstairs wouldn't be able to hear a thing; I didn't need him getting bent out of shape if Trey yelled out.)

6. Bore five holes through his upper lip using the ice pick.

7. Rest, and pound a few shots of vodka.

8. Bore the remaining five holes into his lower lip.

9. Have the large needle ready and threaded with black yarn. (I'd gone to Craft Corral and picked up both the needle and the yarn.)

10. Sew Trey's mouth shut.

Some plans have a way of eating away at you until you do something about them. Writing out the orderly list had been perversely relaxing. Somehow, having a plan physically outside of me helped. Listing each step on paper felt transformative, like purging a poison or having a good long piss.

Aaron's warning that I didn't know enough, the warning he'd given me when he'd seen me at Balk's Hardware, wasn't going to stop me. Even though he'd looked at the ice pick I'd been holding and knew what I was planning, even though he'd said I didn't know enough, I was sticking with my plan. Besides, Aaron was a cross-dressing, exhibitionist pothead, probably a hardcore junkie, so what were the odds he knew anything accurate?

After working through my plan, I treated myself to a beer at Barney's. I took my car just to make sure it ran okay, since I hadn't driven it since the accident.

When I walked in, I noticed my regular seat at the bar was taken, so I settled for a small table at the back. Before heading over, I got a beer from Jason, who greeted me with his usual head nod. When he slid the beer toward me, he called out over the ruckus, "You're just in time. Trey's on his way over."

It was too loud to respond, so I nodded and headed back to nab the table.

I was reading my texts when I heard Trey's laugh up front. I looked up to see him getting a beer and heading my way. Without looking up from my phone I could see his figure approaching the table.

He slipped into the chair across from me and announced, "Dude, we've lost our ground in this place." Trey was referring to our regular stools at the bar being taken.

Setting down my phone, I agreed, making sure to avoid any regret in my tone. "Seems like it, doesn't it? So you ready for Saturday?" Saturday was his big opening at the gallery. In many ways it would be a big night for me, too.

Trey looked down at his beer and exhaled, "As ready as I'm gonna get. Hey, I meant to ask you..." He looked away as if collecting himself to say something emotionally difficult or embarrassing. "I called my mom, you know, to tell her about the opening, and, well, she told me you'd gone to see her? Is that right?"

Oh fuck. I'd not counted on Duffy telling Trey about my visit to Wayne Manor. I'd had the distinct impression they didn't speak anymore. What could I say? I knew I was caught. There was no way out. I had to admit it point blank.

"After you told me about your sister and how she'd disappeared and all, I... wanted to know more. I know it's weird and shit, but I didn't feel like I could ask you."

Trey interrupted me, trying to let me off the hook. "No worries. Duffy liked you. It's cool. I just thought it was weird."

A rush of relief came over me now that he seemed appeased by my comments. "That's probably why I...Listen, I was going to tell you, eventually."

Trey drank from his beer, but he seemed to be thinking, maybe even worrying. "So Duffy told you about me and Trish?" He looked right at me, and I was caught off guard.

Fuck. She'd told him much more than I'd thought. "Yeah, she mentioned it. She said she wasn't happy about it. Didn't want you and your sister—your *half* sister—hooking up." I didn't know how to finish that last sentence without being so frank, but "hooking up" was all that came to mind at that moment.

Trey drank from his beer. His expression became sad, his eyes heavy and lowered. "Listen, I loved her, okay? We were close. We probably shouldn't have hooked up and shit, but she was older, attractive...and we're so much alike...it shouldn't have gone there. You know, our hooking up was not the smartest thing I've done, but..." He paused and seemed to think about what he was going to say next. "It is what it is. It's over now."

"She got pregnant." I said it without thinking. Maybe I was getting angry at his flippancy, at how easily he explained loving Trish and his relationship, like it hadn't caused problems or hadn't led to terrible consequences, consequences that Trish had had to face. It was a cheap shot, but there was too much at stake to let Trey dismiss his relationship with Trish as simply a hookup.

"Yes, Trish got pregnant. I was going to help her get an..." Trey looked around to see if anyone was listening, but the place was loud and even more crowded than before. "Trish wouldn't do it, she wouldn't abort the babies..."

He stopped, and when I looked at him there were tears forming in his eyes. He was heartbroken; this was no act. But then, how could I know anymore?

I had to clarify. I had to know for sure. "You said babies?"

"She was carrying twins...she would've had twins." Trey looked away into the bar, but his eyes seemed to look past all the people, the wooden tables, the walls, everything. I felt bad for him, but not like I once would have. Mostly my sadness was for Trish, who hadn't deserved any of the cruelty and violence she'd suffered.

If I was going to get more information from him, I needed to dig and stir the emotional pot. The next thing I said came out automatically. "They would have been grey babies."

Trey froze. His face changed suddenly, it became hard and angry. I thought he was going to hit me, but instead he asked, "Where the fuck did you hear that?"

What could I say now? I needed to think quickly. Miraculously, the concept behind his new series came back to me. "Your show. The extremes coming together...the black muting the white, the white diluting the black? Your babies would have been grey."

Trey settled down visibly; I'd managed to save myself. But I still wanted more.

"So what happened to the babies?" It took all my strength to sound neutral.

"She lost them, before she...before she disappeared." Trey drank more from his beer before going on. "Hey, if you don't mind, I need to stay focused on my show, and, ah...talking about all this is pretty fucking upsetting."

"You're right. I suppose this is hard shit to talk about." I counted the seconds before asking the most pressing question of all. "What's going on after your show?"

"Actually, I was going to ask if I could crash at your place afterward," Trey said.

"Yeah, sure. I was sort of expecting you to." Part one of my plan could be scratched off the list.

"Thanks." Trey grinned and seemed relieved.

The worst consequence of the visions wasn't the constant deception it required of me but the seething self hatred it caused. I hated who I'd become: a liar and a violent asshole. What with my beating up well-meaning drivers who inadvertently got into accidents and slamming on some little kid's dad at the park, I hardly recognized myself. The person I once was no longer existed.

You know you're lost when your very own thoughts seem alien to you, when the pictures in your head don't look like they used to. My fantasies turned away from getting laid or maybe getting a girlfriend or building on my freelance work or anything *normal* to wanting nothing more than to mutilate my former best friend.

The best way to put it was that I was morphing into the thing I hated the most: *I* was becoming *Trey*. My plan—driven by a dark part of me I had no idea existed until recently—was to carry out the same act of torture Trey had. It didn't escape me how this made me no better than him. Sure, it was for a different reason, some might say a noble one, but I was going to put him through what he'd done to Trish. Except I was going to let him live.

In my skewed thinking, making Trey live with the scars I would most certainly leave on his face would be a daily reminder of his own evil act. It was the best way—no, it was the *only* way I could imagine living in a world where injustices were prevalent.

Knowing I had the power to dole out karma felt pretty fucking good.

By Friday my level of excitement became unbearable; the anticipation of the opening the next day made me unable to work or sit still. After a rush of energy, I got into my car and drove. Without thinking too much about it, I got on the 10 heading west. The 10 West ultimately ends by feeding into PCH. Although the highway was packed, and the four lanes of highway loaded with cars, I didn't mind. Besides, if I lifted my head high enough, I could look over the tops of cars and see the Pacific Ocean to my left—a large span of blue framed by beige sand, a peaceful and oblivious giant, indifferent to our need to crowd and rush from place to place.

Stopped in traffic all around me were people trying to get home, moms driving kids to some sort of activity, and others headed to do whatever else Angelinos did after work. When I looked inside the other cars and saw everyday normal people doing everyday normal things, a feeling of superiority flushed through me. Maybe I didn't drive a convertible Porsche like the old guy next to me or have a hot wife and cute kids like the SUV in front of me, but I was going to do something much bigger. I was going to settle a karmic shift, an inequality that only I could reconcile.

A loud honk behind me woke me from my thoughts. I hit the accelerator and sped ahead until I got to Temescal Canyon Road, where I turned left into a parking lot. It was a large lot and mostly empty at this time of year, but I still drove away from the restaurant it served and headed toward a deserted section.

Leaving my car near a dumpster, I got out and walked toward the long stretch of fawn-colored sand so characteristic of California. What I wanted was to sit, let the ocean do the work, let the rolling waves hypnotize and lull me into a relaxed state. Focusing on this goal alone, I found a cement bench and began the "unwork" of sitting still and allowing.

I was beginning to feel relaxed and good when my phone vibrated in my pocket, which startled the fuck out of me. It pissed me off more than it should have, and when I pulled it out, read the screen, and saw it was Rache, I felt better. Finally she'd called back. But, with a swell of pride and resentment, I let it go to voice mail. She owed me a few; I'd call her back later. For now, sitting and watching the sun drop into the western edge of the world was all I needed.

As peaceful as it all looked, there was a nagging thought that wouldn't go away. Trey said Trish had lost the twins. He hadn't said how, just that she'd lost them. But he'd also said she'd not aborted them; he distinctly said Trish wouldn't do it. If not, then how had they died? Had they died while she'd been struggling in the tub, or had they died naturally in some type of miscarriage? Or if not while in the tub or through natural causes, had they died later, when he'd bludgeoned her in that dark and muggy basement?

The waves were getting bigger and more violent. Far off in the distance, near the horizon, I noticed a dark speck, which could have been anything—a man's head, a pelican, or even a dolphin's fin. As I watched more intently, I noticed the speck wasn't moving, so it couldn't have been a fish. It bobbed involuntarily in the water until a gathering swell lifted it up and dropped it downward in a rolling motion.

The thought it could've been a man, a man in trouble, disturbed me. If he'd seen me and been too weak to call for help, he would've perished alone in the water while I wondered what he was. No matter, the speck— now clearly a buoy—was becoming harder and harder to see as the swells got bigger and crashed more violently, causing a booming sound when they did.

As the waves became more violent and louder, a haunting question came back, one I'd gone out of my way not to consider because of the horror of it. But now, with my defenses down, it returned to haunt: Had Trey bored holes into and sewn Trish's vagina shut? And was that how the babies had died? Had they died sewn inside their mother's womb with no chance to be born, no chance for life? Even after all I'd witnessed during the visions, this thought caused my heart to speed with an anxiety that struck deep.

I shot up from the bench, hoping to wipe the thoughts and images from my mind. If I kept moving, perhaps they'd go away. I trudged through a span of sand back toward the lot where I'd left my car.

There was no more relaxing once those thoughts returned, along with the all-too-real images of Trish's wide-open eyes, the blood smeared and splattered on the tub walls, the black yarn sewn through the skin of her lips. Without another look back at the still setting sun, I left the beach and the struggling buoy behind. There were things I needed to get done before Trey's opening.

———————————————

The cell phone was ringing far off somewhere. At first it seemed like I was dreaming the sound, but then I felt the phone vibrate next to my arm. I must have fallen into a deep sleep, when I'd only meant to nap. I reached around in the covers for it, found it, and squinted to read its face—Rache.

Why was she calling so damn late? I pressed the accept button, but after my sleepy hello, there was no answer. I said it louder and sat up in bed. I could hear people talking on the other end, and I was about to hang up, when a voice called out, "Can you hear me?"

"Rache? Rache? Where are you?"

"This isn't Rache, it's Jessica, her sister..."

"Jess? Why're you calling so late? Is Rache okay?" The time on my phone said 3:22 a.m. Jess lived in Copenhagen, I remembered suddenly, realizing it wasn't late for her, it was daytime.

"You've been calling her, texting her..."

Jessica was why Rache went to Copenhagen after we broke up. She'd gone to regroup, chill, and help out with Jessica's two kids for a while. I'd never met Jessica, but all I'd heard about her were good things. Rache loved and looked up to her older sister.

"Jessica?" I said.

She was crying. She inhaled suddenly in the deep way people do when they cry and are out of breath. Suddenly I knew something bad had happened.

"Jessica, please. What is it? What's happened? I just saw her..."

Jessica sniffled and caught her breath, and when she finally spoke, her voice was shaky. "Saw her?"

"She was here, like two weeks ago…She looked fine." Then I wondered how and why Jessica had Rache's phone. Rache must have gone back to Denmark, to Jessica's place, after I saw her. "Jessica, how did you get her phone?"

Jessica wasn't speaking. I could hear her sobs, her attempts to catch her breath, and each one was like a blow to me. Each one was undeniable evidence that Rachel was gone. It was an unbearable place to be, me wanting answers and Jessica too traumatized to speak or answer my questions.

Then she finally calmed down enough to say, "She never went back to the states. She went straight to Nairobi. The van she was in ran off a hillside. You're wrong."

"No, Jessica, Rache was here. We drank beer, talked…I touched her. She was here." This made her cry even harder. My tone was pretty forceful, but what kind of shit was this?

"Rachel has been in Africa for three weeks. She signed up with a humanitarian group over there and…and, I'm sorry…I needed to tell you. Mom wanted to but…it was too hard for her. She's too broken up, she's not well… I've gotta go, I'm so, so sorry."

"Jessica? Don't go—Jessica?"

She hung up. The screen on my phone darkened. I sat up in bed just as a hard shiver went up my spine. All I could do was stare into my dark bedroom. There was no way Rachel hadn't been here. It was all so real. *It was her.* Fuck that shit, she'd been here.

The pitch blackness of my room was both unnerving and comforting. At least this was real, I told myself. This darkness couldn't be doubted, like my visions, like watching Trey kill, or like having my ex-girlfriend sit next to me while we talked.

Rache dead? This was hard for me to accept, to get my head around.

Could Rache have been a vision too? If so, what part of anything was real?

My heart was pounding, my hands were shaking, and a sweat was beginning to form on my brow. How could this not be real? What was happening to me?

Once again I considered my sanity and my hold on reality. How could I or anyone know for sure if their view of reality was accurate? If it wasn't, how was it I was operating normally in the world? Okay, maybe I'd beat up some guys, but otherwise, I didn't feel at odds with my logical thinking abilities or my capacity to distinguish dreams from truth.

I lay back on my pillow and allowed the news of Rachel's death to sink in. It was too hard to believe she was really gone, that I'd never see her again. Just after finding a niche for us, a newfound friendship, Jess calls to say she's dead, pretty much saying Rache's visit never happened.

It was all too weird and impossible. But then so were the visions, and those I had evidence to prove. Oh fuck, poor Rachel, dead in a far off country. Had she found a way to visit me, to comfort me after her death?

There was no other explanation. Rache had come to see me. She'd found me somehow and come to me. She must have needed to work out our relationship, to set the ground for a peaceful friendship before dying. She was like that. Rache cared about my feelings. She would definitely find a way to come see me, in any physical form she could muster, just to set things straight between us before going away for good.

It was the only possible explanation.

After the call from Jessica, I lay in bed wide awake and unable to relax or sleep. So when the first glimmer of daylight turned the brown curtains yellow, I stripped down, left my clothes in a pile on the floor, and headed toward the shower, trying to forget Rache's visit and how devastated Jessica's voice had sounded over the phone.

The shock of Rachel's death would have to wait, as much as I cared about her, today was Saturday, the day of Trey's gallery opening, and I needed to stay focused.

In the shower, I was surprised when the warm water streaming from the showerhead started to get me hard. It had been a long time since I'd had a hard-on or even thought about masturbating. With my slightly achy and bruised hand, I squeezed my cock until it grew harder and bigger, picturing myself with Trish—a completely fabricated image of Trish as I imagined she'd be, fully grown, unscathed by Trey—but the memory of her in the tub shot right back, as if to reprimand, causing my erection to immediately dwindle. A little frustrated, but not worried, I dried off, put on jeans and a T-shirt, and rushed to get some food in me.

There were only a few menial tasks left to get ready for my work tonight. I'd planned out everything that needed to be done. The hardest part would be going to Trey's show and acting the good friend. It was the one last time I'd have to act natural or hold back around Trey. To be honest, it was getting harder and harder to hold back from telling him how much I hated him and spew out that I knew everything.

I emptied out my freezer to make more room for the bags of ice crowded inside. The ritual of tossing out my frozen shit into a Hefty bag felt awesome. Such a simple act was freeing in a symbolic way, almost like cementing a pact with a friend or fulfilling a promise. Everything but the ice had to go, and once my task was completed, I cinched the bag without a second look and carried it out of my apartment.

As soon as I was outside, I noticed Katherine, the old Russian lady, out with her black dog. They stood across the street, Katherine holding the leash while the little guy hunched over and took a dump.

This had to be real, I told myself. As if daring myself, I called out to Katherine, something I hadn't done in months. "How old is your little guy?"

Katherine squinted in my direction but didn't say anything, so I asked louder. "How old is your dog?"

Squinting up at me again, she said, "Tsarina is a she, she's eight."

I smiled back and nodded. Sure it was strained, a weird attempt at interaction, but it was real. It was real because Katherine heard me and answered.

Lugging the overstuffed and ready-to-burst Hefty bag full of useless and outdated Hot Pockets, frozen peas, ice cream, and whatever else had been in my freezer out back to the dumpster, I saw Stan, my downstairs neighbor. I was so high on life that I actually smiled and greeted him.

"Hey, man, sorry about the noise the other day," I said just as he was about to climb into his car.

He stopped, looked around, finally saw me, and smiled. "Screw it, no worries."

For the first time in a long time, I felt good about things. I had a purpose, and there was no stopping me from success. It was like having a good, clean coke high or an awesome flying dream. I felt invincible.

Back in the kitchen I went about packing and stacking the bags of ice in my freezer, wondering if this was how Trey felt when he'd prepared Trish's torture. How many of his steps was I recreating? A chill of anticipation made me smile; I couldn't wait to have Trey

here and see his face when I told him I knew about Trish, about the grisly torment he'd imposed on his own sister. I couldn't wait to savor the look on his face when I explained that I was going to recreate the nightmare he'd put her through.

As I cleaned up around my apartment, I tried to wipe out the memory of Rache's visit, but I couldn't. There was no way I was going to believe she hadn't been here, right next to me on that very couch just a couple of weeks before.

One thing I was still confused about was how she knew about the pink phone I'd seen in the second vision. I was more certain now that I'd not mentioned it. Maybe she'd brought it up as a way to let me know she knew more than she'd let on. What baffled me was how she'd talked me into believing

Trey was incapable of murder and a coverup. It was clear Rache had belived him innocent, going so far as to ask why I hadn't called the police if I'd been so sure he was a killer.

A friend of mine once told me about accounts of people having seen, touched, and spoken to love ones after they'd died. She'd explained the principles of energy, of how energy couldn't be destroyed or created but was transformed from one state to another. She'd argued the principle could be applied to souls. If so, it was absolutely possible that Rachel's soul had transported itself here, to be with me.

Once I got my place cleaned up, I showered, shaved, and dressed. Before leaving for Trey's opening, I made sure to fill the bathtub halfway. I figured his weight along with the ice would displace any additional water.

Before heading out the door, I brought Trish's painting into the living room and set it against the television. That way, when Trey came in, it would be the first thing he'd see. How better to introduce the subject than one of his sister's paintings staring up at him?

EIGHTH STITCH

WHEN YOU TURN THE CORNER FROM Santos—a relatively quiet residential street—onto Melrose, it's like switching on lights in a dark room. You go from the little stimulation of sleepy, treelined streets to an onslaught of lights, cars, people, smells, and the welcome sense of disappearing into a crowd.

Alone but surrounded by others had become my default state. There was no one left that I could turn to about anything I'd been experiencing, no one to confide in about the visions. The brief sense of relief of having Rache to confide in had been stripped from me. It was an empty and soulless feeling, to be so alone, but one I could grow accustomed to, if need be.

Everything I would do tonight, I would do for Trish. But there was something more that drove me. The thought of hurting Trey was more pleasurable than anything else I could think of. Most people would think it weird. Of course they would, but then they hadn't had to suffer through the visions, to look pain and death square in the face while frozen in place without any chance to stop it.

The closer I got to the CW Gallery, the louder the music got. Even from across the street where I stood, the pumping bass and the crowd gathered outside called attention to the space. Before crossing over, I tried looking through the plate-glass windows for a glimpse of Trey, but all I could see were people teeming inside the gallery, blocking the view inside. Not one of them did I recognize. In fact, from where I was, they all looked fake, like made-to-order gallery-opening attendees. There were several fedora-wearing wannabe hipsters floating about, several heads sporting bushy dreads, and a few Che Guevara berets. I'd never hated the art world so much as I did at that moment. So many dickheads.

I crossed the street and smelled the sweet smell of clove cigarettes coming from a group of smokers gathered outside the entrance like a wolf pack. I didn't stop or slow down to see if I knew any of them.

Standing on the sidewalk, I looked through the squeaky-clean gallery window. Through the bodies ambling inside I caught a glimpse, mostly a flash, of one of Trey's new paintings through the window, but it didn't register. Maybe I was too nervous or distracted, but I didn't notice anything odd about his new series. Not yet anyway.

It suddenly struck me that, as prepared as I was for dealing with Trey after the show, I'd not prepared myself for being at the actual opening. Sure I'd organized everything else—even fantasized about it—but I'd not given much thought to what it would be like once I was there.

From where I stood at the window, through the shifting groups of people, a partial wall was visible. The wall, not much larger than a tall and elongated pedestal, had a large, framed image displayed on it. But some dude in a dark grey suit and green sneakers suddenly stood directly in front of me, blocking my view of it. He was talking to one of the dreadlocked chicks, and I almost pounded on the window to get them to move.

Instead of making a scene, I inched over on the sidewalk and got a quick view of the wall just when a group of people separated, leaving an open hole through which I could see the enlarged black-and-white photograph of Trish. She was smiling but not really looking into the camera or even toward whoever had taken the shot. She was looking up, as if she'd seen a bird behind the photographer and was following its flight. Her smile wasn't full either; it was the type of half smile people got when deep in thought, distracted, or slightly worried. Below the photograph was a statement or a tribute, but I couldn't make out the words.

It was time for me to go in, check out the art, and see if the fuss over Trey's series was more than just fuss. As soon as I opened the door, a draft of cold air conditioning hit my face, the ruckus of too many voices irked my hearing, and the smell of fresh paint irritated my sense of smell. Above all, and most disturbing, was being struck, once again, by the faraway sound of Trish's voice.

There were about eighty, maybe a hundred people crowded into the two-thousand-square-foot space, and their separate voices, conversations, and bursts of laughter came at me in one collective mumble. Part of me wanted to yell out at the top of my lungs for all of them to shut the fuck up so I could peacefully listen to the static recording of Trish reading her poetry.

As nervous and shaken as I already was, I was hit by a fucking swell of emotions. Maybe it was the sound system playing her voice so clearly and pristinely, making it seem like she was whispering in my ear, whispering her fears in the melodramatic code of poets, because I found myself holding back tears.

Fuck. I'd been standing at the entrance holding the front door open and staring, for how long I couldn't say. All I knew was that people were turning around to look at me. I couldn't risk losing it here, not with all these assholes staring. Then I saw Trey standing in the center of the room with a drink in his hand and a strange relaxed grin on his face. Smugness is what I saw, plain and simple. From the look of him, he wasn't listening to Trish's poetry. He was too busy being the badass artist everybody wanted to meet. Her words meant nothing to him. It was crystal clear that the only thing that mattered to Trey was the idea or the concept of Trish. He used the public tragedy of her loss like paint on a canvas; its only purpose was to help him express a feeling, a sentiment, and a loss. It was effective, but without care or concern for Trish, the result was rancid and no more moral or right than using starving children to elicit a reaction or to sell a product.

> *Two grey,*
> *Tightly woven,*
> *Bound and gagged,*
> *Umbilically corded,*
> *Souls,*
> *One loved,*
> *One not*

The poem was spelling so much out. Bound and gagged? Two souls, one loved one not? Hadn't Trey listened to the poems before airing them so cavalierly? Part of me wanted to stand in place, to not move and only listen to her words. More than anything I wanted to tune out the other voices, the people milling about, even Trey. It was maddening that while I gave credence to Trish's work, everyone else ignored it. This alone both baffled and enraged me.

The entry where I stood didn't allow me to see any of the paintings, so I had to push my way through groups of bodies to finally get to a wall. The nearer I got to the first wall of art, the more my heart began to pound. Why was I feeling so ill at ease? Something was wrong; I could feel it. The first painting I saw was from afar, but it was enough for me to see what Trey had done.

As I neared the first wall, a couple stood directly in front of the canvas and blocked my view, but over their heads and on the wall next to them I saw the plastic baby dolls so characteristic of Trish's work. I couldn't believe it. I blinked and tried making visual sense, tried rationalizing what I was looking at, which could only amount to one thing—Trey was showing Trish's work as his own.

Everywhere I looked, plastered over every single wall space in the gallery, were Trish's paintings. Grey, bound baby dolls with mouths and genitals sewn shut in black yarn.

The same artist who'd painted the canvases Duffy had shown me had painted these, and it was Trish. Then it came back to me: when Duffy had given me Trish's painting back at Wayne Manor, she'd said, "Take this. You'll need it."

It took me a few seconds to let it sink in, for me to piece together Trey's enormous ability to deceive. What's more, it struck me that Trey didn't know I'd seen Trish's work; as far as he was concerned, he was getting away with plagiarism.

Now I knew why Duffy thought I'd need the painting, why she'd been so insistent on my taking it. Duffy must have known Trey was showing Trish's work as his own. It explained why she hadn't attended the opening. It also explained why Trey and Duffy were on the outs. Later, when I confronted Trey, the painting would be undeniable proof that I was onto him. I was pleased with myself, pleased I'd set the painting out prominently in my apartment for Trey to see.

If emotions could be physical entities—things with size, force, and vigor—mine, at that moment, were of galactic strength. It felt like a black hole was forming inside me, sucking me in and away from all things normal and shifting me toward a hateful place were lies were truth and people you thought were your friends were killers.

I hadn't thought about talking to anyone or even speaking much at Trey's opening. I'd mentally worked out very little besides coming in, showing my face, checking out the art, and then making an exit. Fuck, the last thing I thought I'd do was yell out and address everyone in the gallery in a feeble attempt to expose Trey's plagiarism, but that's what I did.

"Trey!" I called, but the excited, alcohol-fueled din in the room was stubborn and hard to break. One guy turned around to look at me briefly, but turned back to his conversation. So I called out in a forceful, angry holler, "*Hey Trey!*" The room got suddenly quiet. Now it was just me and Trish talking. I heard her saying, "Take piece after piece of me," right before I howled again.

"What are you doing?" I asked, approaching him where he stood, open mouthed and shocked in the center of the now very quiet gallery. Without meaning to, I bumped some chick on the way, causing her to spill her drink. She turned and gave me a hard look like she was ready to cuss me out, but when she saw my rage-face, she got out of the way.

The space grew still; people had stopped in place to observe the commotion. It was too quite, so quite I wondered if I'd lost my ability to hear, just like in the visions. But then I heard my footsteps, a guy clearing his throat somewhere in the gallery, and someone whispering. As I got closer to where Trey stood, it struck me that someone had turned off the soundtrack. Now it was just me talking without the comfort of Trish's words to urge me on.

"You're a fuckin' plagiarist."

I heard a few people shift in place uncomfortably. A few others walked toward the back of the gallery.

"Why don't you tell them, Trey? Why not mention that none of this is *your work?*"

I didn't know it yet, but when I caught my reflection on the window behind Trey, I saw that I was smiling. It felt awesome to yell out the truth, to force Trey to face his deception. I was free, I was the one guy tilting the universe back into orbit, making things right. Yeah, me.

"I think you owe these people an explanation." My finger was on the edge of the world, tipping things back into place. "Don't you think *they should know* you didn't paint these?" I laughed, knowing I risked sounding like the typical crazy guy in some cheesy story, but I couldn't help it. It felt so good.

Trey looked scared. His eyes met mine, and when I saw fear, I savored the moment, allowing the quiet in the room to crawl over and crowd Trey. Fuckhead had it coming.

The next move was his. I'd said all I had to say. The ball was on his side of the court. Then, from out of nowhere, some asshole grabbed my arms from behind and yanked me backward, almost knocking me off balance. As he dragged me away from Trey, he hoisted me up just before I could fall to the floor.

Whoever he was, he was stronger and taller than me. But somehow I was able to pull my left arm out of his grip. I raised my arm and pointed at the walls. "Tell them, Trey. Tell them how you mutilated Trish…how you killed her and the grey babies…"

I yelled as loud as I could, but now I was competing with the clamor of people talking to each other in worried tones, no doubt pointing and wondering how a wackjob like me had made it into the show. No one was listening anymore. To all these people I was just some crazed guy, or a jealous colleague of Trey's who'd acted out.

The unseen guy behind me tightened his grip on my arms and pulled my shoulders back in a painful and unnatural angle. He dragged me out onto the sidewalk, past the smokers, around the side of the building, and into a back alley. But I never once stopped my truth rant. I yelled out louder and louder the farther we got. He pulled me backward so fast that the only way I could remain upright was to kick out my feet to keep pace with him.

He stopped pulling me when we were deep into the red brick alley. The surroundings and the guys—because now that I could see, I noticed that another huge guy had joined the one who'd roughed me out of the gallery—looked so cliché, the brick alley so like a bad movie that I laughed at the ridiculousness of it all. This, though, was a mistake, because the one guy, the white one, gritted his teeth (also a pretty funny cliché) before knocking me around pretty hard and slamming me against the wall of the alley.

My head thumped against the brick wall behind me, and all the humor and hilarity I'd had disappeared. The guys were not only tall but hugely muscular in an unnaturally steroidal way, which only scared me more. The white one smiled, as if he enjoyed his work. The black one frowned like he meant business.

Now that we were away from public view, the black guy grabbed me by the arm and tossed me to the ground. I wasn't hurt so much as disoriented as I watched him climb on me, straddle me, just before pulling his fist back to slam my face. I heard my cheek crack before passing out.

When I came to and opened my eyes, I was still on the ground. The familiar soundtrack must have been turned back on inside the gallery, because I heard it pounding and reverberating off the walls of the alley. The two guys were standing about four feet away from where I lay. They faced one another and talked loudly in bickering tones.

The black one said, "Just call the fuckin' cops."

Fuck, cops were the last people I wanted to deal with. It wasn't being arrested that bothered me, it was the time it would take. If I was taken into custody, which looked likely, they'd take me downtown, question me, and hold me until Trey or the gallery owner decided whether or not to press charges. I would run out of time, and my whole plan would be ruined.

That thought alone took about a split second to race through my head. It prompted me to scramble up onto my feet, stumble around the two fuckheads, and sprint away as fast and hard as I could.

"Fuckin' pussy. You better run," one of the guys called out behind me. They laughed in unison while I ran, and since I didn't hear any footsteps pursuing me, it was obvious they were glad to be rid of me. It was better this way; if the cops came, they'd have to explain my cracked cheek, bleeding nose, and the fragments of teeth floating around in my mouth.

It was getting dark now, and even though I wasn't being chased, I ran east on Melrose as if the two guys were right behind me. It must have looked weird to see me, a bleeding guy in a torn shirt running down the street, weaving around people on dates, headed to comedy clubs, restaurants, or bars. It must have been even weirder to see that guy laughing hard, because I was.

A high had come over me for the first time in months. Just after getting away from the dickheads, an unnatural euphoria swept through me like a chill with goose bumps. Fuck, I'd told Trey everything! I'd caught him at his own sick game, and even though the people at the gallery thought I was crazy, Trey knew I'd caught him. Trey knew every word I'd said was true.

The look of culpability in his eyes was all I needed; he was trapped and he knew it. Missing from his expression was remorse; I hadn't noticed a speck of that. Still, that I'd come clean after months of holding in all I knew—all the cruelty I'd witnessed—felt liberating. I was giddy with it. Fuck felt good.

While running, the chill night air cooled my skin. It also dried what must've been a lot of blood on my face. The more air that struck my cheek, the more contracted and puckered my skin felt as the blood dried and crusted.

My plan was still the same—head home and wait for Trey. There was no way he'd not come over now. He'd want an explanation. He'd want to know how I'd recognized Trish's paintings. He'd want answers. I'd relax with a little weed and vodka and wait for him to show.

What I wished I had was some Vicodin left over from my hand injury, but I didn't. I'd taken the last few for kicks, had wasted them on getting off. The dreamlike sensation it offered so nicely didn't seem as important now that I faced unavoidable pain. Although I wasn't hurting yet, it wouldn't be long until my face began to throb in an overture to the intense pain that would follow.

Since I was only a few blocks from Flaco's and his setup at Martha's Mom, I headed there. When I slowed down my pace into a brisk walk, I began to notice the wide-eyed, surprised looks I got from people. Melrose was crowded, which made not bumping into people almost impossible; I heard a few angry comments when I inadvertently struck shoulders or swiped someone's side. "Bloody fuck. Watch where you're going, Gap fag," being the most memorable and oddly entertaining.

Out of breath and still on my excitement high, I stood outside Flaco's shop and caught my breath. My cheek began to pound. At least for now the pounding was just that, a painless throb, but I knew I was up against the clock and running out of time before the throb took on a bite.

As I paced back and forth on the sidewalk in front of the large window, I focused on catching my breath before walking in. Also, if Flaco had a customer, I would have to wait for them to leave, because asking for Vicodin or any other shit that wasn't legal weed would put him on the spot, get him reported, or worse, cost him his license.

Getting a look into Martha Mom's was tough though. Unlike normal storefront windows, Martha's had a ton of crap blocking the view from outside. Getting even a small glimpse into the place involved a lot of neck craning to see over and around the haphazard displays. Flaco had done the work on his own, and what he called décor was no more than scattered litter.

With my cheek pounding out the rhythm of my heartbeat, I stood up on my toes with my head raised so I could see past the dusty hookah pipes, decorative bongs, and a fading *Scarface* poster. Just as I did, one thing became grossly evident: Flaco was being held up.

Some guy, who wasn't identifiable behind the hoodie covering his head, stood facing Flaco, who stared at the gun pointed at him. The guy must have said something, because Flaco, who'd been still, suddenly began rushing around behind the counter. He looked near tears as he hurried to place all kinds of crap into a big white plastic bag. The guy in the hoodie kept using the gun to point at shit he wanted while poor Flaco did all he could to be quick about following orders.

Where was his trusty weekend security guard, Drew? Slowly walking nearer to the front door, I looked around inside as best I could for him, but there was no sign of the big guard. I wondered if he'd gone out or taken the night off. Fuck, Flaco needed him *now*.

Searching my front pocket in vain for my phone, it hit me I'd left it in my car back home to charge. My only recourse was to go somewhere else for help. The small coffeehouse next door always had people inside, so I rushed in and went straight to the girl behind the counter.

"Hey, I need help!"

She didn't look up or pay any mind to my excitement. Instead she seemed concerned with holding the coffee cup just so under a loud espresso machine.

Raising my voice to make sure she could hear me over the damn machine, I said, "You gotta call the cops! Flaco is being held up next door!" The girl, whose cheek was pierced with four huge rings, looked bored and still didn't seem to register the danger Flaco was in, so I said it again. "Call the fucking police!"

Just then she set down the cup, walked over to the phone on the counter, and lifted the receiver. But she didn't call right off. For the first time she actually looked at me and asked, "So it's a 911 call, right?"

"Yes, that's right." It was all I could say. There was no use in my complicating things for her.

It wasn't until I turned from the all-too-bored girl at the counter that the throb in my cheek pounded into the first pang of an intensely sharp pain.

———————◆———————

Running back home was impossible. Each time my foot struck the ground, a sharp pain shot up my face, and so walking was all I could handle. But even that wasn't much better. I kept wondering and hoping Flaco had come out of the holdup unscathed, but I wouldn't know for sure, not until this night was well past me. For now all I could think of was getting home and getting as much Tylenol, ibuprofen, and vodka in me as I could. There was time, plenty of time, before Trey came over.

When I got to my building, there was a shiny new Mercedes parked out front, which was unusual. Next to it, and standing directly in front of the entrance to my apartment, was a woman. Could it be Aaron out to contact me again? Taking to the shadowy part of the sidewalk, I slowed my pace to get a better look.

The closer I got, the more I made out the woman's girth and the unmistakable puffy blonde hair: Duffy. She was pacing and smoking a cigarette, obviously impatient and obviously waiting for me. Why else would she be standing outside my building?

Just as I was about to turn and head the other way, she saw me. She dropped her cigarette on the sidewalk and walked toward me. Fuck, there was no escaping her. I needed to get into my apartment for painkillers, and even if I managed to get around her, there wasn't a back way into my place. Facing her was unavoidable.

Duffy stared at me with a weird expression. The closer I got, the more she cocked her head and squinted. Finally it dawned on me what my face must have looked like—what a bloodied, smashed-in mess it had to be.

"Aaron was at the opening. He told me everything," Duffy explained without any prompting. Then she paused, got a better look at me, and frowned. "What the fuck happened to you?"

Of course she meant my bashed-in face, but I ignored her. I was way too pissed. "Aaron was there, was he? He must have missed the thorough beating I got in the back alley, I guess." I didn't wait for an answer. "So I take it you and Aaron are okay with Trey passing Trish's work off as his own?"

Duffy looked at me sadly. I mean this. She looked heartbroken, devastated. "Of course not. It's wrong, but it's not what you think."

This was too much. I rushed her and got in her face. I couldn't help it. "Yeah, really now? You know what I think? Trey fucking mutilated his own sister...killed her, killed the babies, and now he's showing her paintings. Am I close, Duffy?"

Duffy was crying, just like I figured she would.

"I'm calling the police, you got that? They need to know about Trey. Fuck, somebody has to do the right thing."

With my keys in hand, I walked past Duffy and was about to unlock the gate leading into the courtyard when she spoke out. I'd been bluffing about calling the cops, but she didn't know that. At this point all I really wanted was to carry out my plan. The last thing I needed was to ruin things by reporting Trey tonight. The thought of all the shit that went with reporting a crime wasn't in tonight's schedule. Fuck no. I'd managed to avoid the police twice in one night, I wasn't about to succumb now. It was payback time, and the only thing left was to get Duffy to leave so I could wash down a handful of Tylenol with vodka and wait for Trey.

"If you come back with me, I'll show you everything you need to know. But I need you to not call the police." She looked so sincere when she said this that I stopped in place and waited to hear more. She looked away as if gathering her strength before going on. "I'm just trying to protect my family. I'm angry at Trey for showing Trish's work, yes, but you're wrong about him."

"Why should I trust you, Duffy? The way I see it, you'd rather I shut up and went away."

"I guess there's no reason why you should trust me."

She paused and looked around, as if gathering strength to speak. In the streetlight, Duffy looked old and worn out. The fat in her face weighed on her cheeks, dragging them downward as opposed to filling them out. Her hair, a brittle mass that lacked shine or luster, looked dry and lifeless even in the dim lighting.

She raised a hand to wipe away the tears on her face, and she exhaled deeply before continuing. "Listen, I'm risking a lot by reaching out to you. I'm risking the only family I have left. I'll be exposing everything and then hoping you understand enough to let things go. Please, just come to the house with me."

There was an earnestness in her voice that convinced me to listen, to give her a chance. Besides, Trey's show would go on until late, so I had time to head to Wayne Manor with Duffy and still be back with time to spare.

Without missing a beat, I clarified things just to be sure I was in control. "We drive separate cars, I leave when I want, and if you try anything funny, I call the police and report Trey immediately."

While I was setting down the rules, one selfish thought coursed through my mind—Duffy, of all people, was the best person for me to be with after all. She would have a shitload of painkillers. Who else was I going to score kick-ass painkillers from but her? The pain was bad now, but it was going to get worse, and when Trey was over, I'd need all my strength.

"I'm going to need stuff for my pain. Strong shit." I put it out there, just to be sure.

Duffy looked at my cheek and nodded before saying, "Yes, you will. So follow me."

With that, I agreed to follow Duffy to Wayne Manor.

She waited out front while I went straight back to the carport and got my car. When I drove out from the back, Duffy was already in her car and waiting. Once she saw my car, she pulled out and drove while I followed.

Driving behind her, I focused on the curved red taillights of her Mercedes without paying much attention to the road. At the first stop sign, I glanced at my cell sticking out of the center console. It was now fully charged and showing a text from Tina, most likely about the illustrations, which I'd have to deal with later. I switched the power off, both to extend the battery life and to avoid any unnecessary distractions for the rest of the evening.

It had been a nonstop, weird, action-movie type of night so far, and being able to sit, drive, and regroup was a godsend. At a stoplight I ventured a look at myself in the rearview mirror and almost laughed at how bad I looked. There was dried blood around my mouth, creating a Joker-like look, one of my front teeth was chipped, my right eye was beginning to swell, and the first signs of bruising were starting to show. No wonder I'd gotten all those weird looks.

As I got onto the 134 heading east, Duffy's Mercedes sped away and disappeared into the mass of red taillights. My car was no match, so I flipped on the radio and did my best to unwind.

The added resentment I had for Trey after discovering he'd so boldly pla-giarized Trish's work only added to the festering hatred I'd amassed in the last few months. He had some balls showing Trish's paintings like that. I could see having a show featuring her work and attributing it to her posthumously, but flat out claiming it was his was fucked up.

The only way I could reconcile Trey's actions was to assume he'd dismissed any sense of right and wrong a long time ago. His lack of remorse fit right in with the profile of a sociopath. Whatever I did to Trey from here on out, what-ever pain I brought on him, wouldn't be enough.

NINTH STITCH

By the time I got over the canyon and into Glendale, my face was throbbing, my right hand was swelling again, and my teeth ached. I kept cussing at myself for not grabbing a Tylenol or anything before getting in the car and facing the freeway traffic. I blasted the radio and tried to get lost in the music, noticing how the throbbing in my face seemed to match the beat of whatever song played. Every time the sea of red brake lights grew brighter ahead—indicating a slowdown—I panicked, but somehow, maybe because of my focus on the pain, I got to the San Rafael Avenue exit sooner than I expected.

After turning right at the offramp, Duffy's familiar taillights were visible about a block ahead. I followed her through streets with massive, gated estates the size of small villages, where the houses, when visible from the road, looked more like hotels than homes. Before I knew it, we were driving up the equally grand private road that led to the top of Wayne Manor.

As soon as I pulled behind Duffy's car, the pain in my face was so sharp, all I could think of was getting out and rushing her.

"Duffy…my face…it's fucking killing me."

Without looking my way, she nodded and walked inside, and I followed. Every step felt like spikes were being hammered into my face.

Being still and waiting for her was all I had in me. At this point even breathing caused pain. Once in the entry hall, I lowered myself into one of the two throne-like chairs, feeling like a servant awaiting a royal appointment. My thoughts were divided between trying to forget the pain and hoping Duffy would come out with something stronger than aspirin.

Minutes later Duffy appeared, like an angel, a water bottle in one hand, the other holding a dark mustard-colored prescription container. I nearly jumped for joy when she held it out for me, but when I scrambled to open it, the pain and swelling in my hand made it near impossible. In desperation I raised the container up to my mouth and tried biting the fucking lid open with my teeth. Duffy laughed loudly before taking the bottle from me, flipped off the lid with one quick movement, and shook out two lovely, white Vicodin pills into my grateful and anxious palm.

I popped both into my mouth, chewing once to break them up before swigging from the water Duffy had mercifully cracked open for me. My head fell back on the headrest, and I closed my eyes, ready to give up everything for respite from the searing pain pounding away in my cheek and hand. But Duffy wanted me to follow her.

"Come on, it works faster when you aren't waiting for it." She walked out the front door, while I did my best to forget the pain and follow.

Duffy began talking as she charged ahead on the gravel footpath. The loud crunching of her steps drowned out some of her words, so I caught only bits and pieces of what she was saying.

"When you first showed up here…you knew something…wondered if Trey had told you about…disappearance…"

My thoughts were scattered, but not enough to stop me from realizing I couldn't stay here long. Eventually I needed to get back to my place before Trey did.

"I don't need the police to decide what is right for my family. You got that?" Duffy stopped walking. She'd turned to glare at me with a hard and forceful expression. "This is a family issue, do you understand?"

She waited for me to agree, and when I didn't, she added, "The police can't do shit about any of this anyway."

I mumbled back as best I could, since moving my face in any way, even to talk, hurt. "Would Trish say so?"

"You don't know fuck-all about anything." Duffy spat this out before turning and plodding ahead.

We passed the small lake—the replica of the one I'd drawn—now black in the darkness. Somehow it looked wild and less tended without daylight. The mountains behind it were hardly visible and could have been mistaken for looming storm clouds. The rocks on the shore looked solid, as if they'd melded into one huge span, each blending into its neighbor, each indecipherable from the other, as if at night they joined forces to create one.

Part of me wished I wasn't in such a hurry to get back; the sensation of walking through the gardens in the dark was trippy and surreal. The hedged-in gardens, the pale statues set into corners as if posing, and the far-off sound of fountains splashing were beautiful in a haunting way. None of it looked or seemed real. At one point I stopped to touch the base of an unusually tall statue. It was different from the others; not only was it larger, but given its light, nearly white color, I suspected it had been carved from marble.

The statue was of a partially nude, heavily muscled man. His twisted torso and raised arm made it look like he'd been reaching for the sky or for something that had flown from his grasp. The marble base was cold and smooth, and as I rubbed over it, I felt an indentation carved into the stone, but in the dark it was impossible to make out the words. Using my fingers to feel out the letters of the chiseled inscription, I felt an M and an O.

Then, suddenly, Duffy called out from the darkness, "You should see him in the light. He's beautiful…Morpheus, the Greek god of dreams." Duffy had stopped to admire him with me. Then, without another word, she turned and continued on her way, crunching through the gravel while I took one last look at Morpheus.

We walked until we approached a tall structure. The closer we got, the more I knew it had to be the cottage I'd seen in the vision. This was where Duffy had reprimanded poor Aaron, warning him never to bring anyone. Of course, I'd only seen it in a vision, so until now I wasn't sure the building actually existed.

In the darkness the cottage seemed oddly more welcoming and less abandoned than it had in the vision. At roughly four thousand square feet, it looked to be constructed of the same brick and stone used in the main house but scaled down to a smaller size. It seemed too grand to be a groundskeeper cottage, and I wondered if it had originally served as a guesthouse. In the dark I could see light, an amber glow showing through gaps in the boarded-up windows.

I stood staring until Duffy surprised me by grabbing my good hand to lead me past the carved wooden front door to a smaller back door.

Before I could think or stop myself, I said, "The babies—the twins."

Ignoring my comment, Duffy pounded on the door and called out, "Marcel! Marcel, it's me, open up. It's okay!"

I wondered if the babies were alive, if maybe they'd been spared somehow. If they were, then Trey had been lying about Trish having lost them. That was no surprise. Trey's lying was becoming commonplace. But they wouldn't be babies anymore. Hell, they'd be kids by now. Besides, why would Duffy hide them away in a back cottage? What was the point of that?

The door opened and an older, grey-haired man appeared. He walked outside and closed the door behind him. He seemed scared, uncomfortable even. He looked at me briefly then at Duffy.

"Miss Duffy, what you doing? This is not right interrupting so late. It upsets the schedule."

Marcel's English was broken and had an indistinguishable accent, possibly European but hard to pinpoint. I wondered why he was disturbed by Duffy's visit, when she so clearly seemed to run the whole place. One thing was for sure: Marcel was extremely uncomfortable with my being there; he kept shooting panicky glances my way when he thought I wasn't looking.

"How is he? Is he having a quiet night?" Duffy asked, but Marcel just looked at me. It became very clear it wasn't about me; *anyone* being here at this hour was suspect. Duffy lost her patience now. "He's my son, Marcel. I don't care how late it is. It's my decision. Now let us in."

Her son?

Marcel hesitantly turned around and walked in first. He held the door open for us. I followed Duffy, not knowing what to expect, not really sure I wanted to be here anymore. We walked into a small but brand new and well-lit kitchen. Compared to the mystery and darkness of the exterior of the cottage, this space seemed ordinary and regular—a place where everyday activities took place, and my apprehension began to fade.

By now the Vicodin was beginning to do its work. The receptors that had so aptly registered my injuries were being blocked and numbed. The pain was becoming a memory. An added advantage was that Vicodin tended to quiet my moods. It now quelled the anxiety, which had trailed me like a shadow since I'd left the gallery.

Duffy stormed past the kitchen and into an adjoining room. I stayed behind, unsure of what to do. I stood, while Marcel took a chair at a long wooden table without once looking away from me. After a bit, I heard Duffy speaking to someone in the other room, but as hard as I listened, I couldn't make out any voice but hers. She spoke in lowered tones, so I couldn't tell what she was saying until she called out, much louder, "You can come in."

Marcel gestured for me to go with a dismissive flip of his wrist. I walked toward Duffy's voice, past an unlit butler's pantry separating the kitchen and the room where she was. I heard a fire crackling just as I walked into the small den. Duffy sat on a couch facing the fire, her back to me. I walked around so she could see me, but stopped when I saw Trey sitting on the couch next to her, his head resting on her shoulder.

"What...what's going on?"

Neither Duffy nor Trey answered, which was more annoying than confusing.

"Trey, can you tell me what the fuck is going on?" The nearer I got to where he sat, with his head on Duffy's shoulder, looking like some fucking kid, the more pissed I got. Just as I was about to reach down and grab him, Trey whined or was it a hum? Either way, it didn't sound right; something was wrong.

He smiled and hid his head in his mother's shoulder as if stricken with shyness, which blew me away. Then he spoke, and when he did, he fucking sounded like a bratty kid and not like Trey at all. "I'm *not* Trey."

At that moment, I realized I'd heard the much different voice before. It was the voice Trey took on in my visions. But that this guy sitting before me wasn't Trey was still not registering.

Duffy caressed his head, and all I could do was sit down on a nearby chair. While I openly stared at the spectacle they made, I tried figuring out what was going on.

"So you left your own show, your own fucking opening?" I asked, this time appealing to Duffy.

Duffy met my gaze and in an angry voice said, "This is Matt, his brother."

Matt didn't make eye contact with me; he just kept his head on his mother's shoulder in a peculiar, all too infantile way.

There was something really weird about a guy my age cuddling up to his mother. And while a shitload of questions raced through my head, questions I wanted to ask Duffy, all I could do was stare at this weird guy, who looked exactly like Trey, snuggle his mom. As much as I wanted to ask Duffy questions, I hesitated because of Matt sitting there looking so fucking bizarre. Needless to say, I was totally thrown off.

"Why...I mean...why hasn't Trey ever said anything?" My instinct was to ask Duffy. By now it was clear Matt wasn't all there.

Much later, when I reflected on meeting Matt, it would be easy to see he'd been the logical culprit, the missing piece in Trish's murder, the obvious answer to the puzzle, but while there and after first meeting him, all those things didn't add up so quickly.

As I sat there with both Matt and Duffy looking at me, I was still confused, still working stuff out in my head. It was like being given a nearly solved Rubik's cube: it looks more solved than it really is. One wrong move and you add ten more moves to the puzzle. It was a lot to digest. Sometimes getting the answer to a question all at once can be mind muddling.

"Twins?" This was all I could muster.

Duffy nodded. "Identical. Except for the schizophrenia. Matt was asymptomatic until he was ten or so. Trey is free of it."

"I have a bad disease," Matt started to sing much too loudly. "Up from my head is where I bleeeeed." He sang the Red Hot Chili Peppers song, giving it a much different meaning. He looked up at me and smiled.

A weird chill rushed through me, and I couldn't hold Matt's gaze. It was too hard looking this skinny, sickly, and all-wrong version of Trey in the eyes.

Matt had to be the killer. It had been him in my visions all along. Fuck, all the things I'd thought about Trey weren't true. It'd been this pathetic, mentally deranged guy sitting in front of me the whole time. Matt being the killer made sense, but until now how was I to know?

"So it wasn't Trey who...?"

I needed to ask, and instead of getting an answer from Duffy, Matt jumped up, came to where I sat in the armchair, and got in my face. His cigarette smoker's breath was so strong that I had to turn away. For a second I thought I'd have to shove him off me, but he pulled back a little. He was angry and almost yelled in my face.

"I sewed her up. She did it all the time to her dolls. Right, Mom?" He turned to direct his question at his mother, who I could see was heartbroken but somehow accustomed to his banter.

Matt turned away from me and walked back to plop himself next to his mother on the couch. I tried to get a look at his arm, to see if he had the scars I'd looked for on Trey, but his long-sleeved shirt came down to his wrists.

"Trish and Trey were fuckers...fuck, fuck, fuck..." His tone changed, and his mood seemed to be shifting. Now he seemed more placid, less threatening. I wondered if I should get the hell out now, but I wanted to hear what he had to say much too badly.

"They were fuckers...and fuckers make babies." He lifted his head from his mother's shoulder to ask, "Right?"

He turned back to me. "I saw them. She wouldn't do it with me, only Trey, she said." Matt's face contorted into a painful, red recollection of his unrequited passion, and then he began to cry. He didn't hold back either; his was a child's cry, a high-pitched, full-forced, exaggerated howl.

He kept at it until I stood to leave, then he stopped. Matt seemed suddenly intrigued by me. He raised his head to watch my every move just as unabashedly as a child.

"You're friends with him, aren't you?" Matt's tone changed; he sounded less like a child.

I waited for him to say more, and when he didn't, I answered. "Trey is the closest friend I have," I said. With his gaze still on me, Matt clenched his jaw in an all too familiar way. I'd seen Trey engage in the same jaw-clenching maneuver for years. When Trey got angry or felt insulted, he, too, clenched his jaw.

There was no need to say anything more to Trey's peculiar and downright disturbing doppelganger, so I nodded toward Duffy and headed toward the hall that led back into the kitchen. Once there, I stopped and turned. There was one thing I still needed to see.

"Matt, can you show me your arm?"

From the back of the couch, I saw Matt look at his mother for permission. He waited until she nodded her approval before turning onto his knees and leaning over the back of the couch to face me. He lifted his shirtsleeve up to his elbow. Later, I would remember how he'd not asked which sleeve to lift. It was as if he knew exactly what I'd been looking for.

And there it was, the long, deeply indented scar I assumed he'd have, based on the scratches Trish had caused during her struggle—a struggle I only knew about because I'd seen it transpire in a vision. This very scar had perplexed me for sometime. I'd looked for it on Trey's arm but never found it, and there it was, clear as day, on Matt's. The scar and Matt were the remaining pieces of evidence, the last missing pieces in my struggle to match the visions to the truth.

As I walked away, Duffy called out behind me. "You still need to talk to Trey."

I stopped and looked at her, not sure what she wanted from me. "You mean I owe him an apology?"

"That's up to you."

"What about the babies? What about Trish's ba—"

Duffy jumped off her seat, startling Matt, who shifted to avoid being struck by her big body. She turned to give me a hard, threatening look meant to quiet me. Apparently she thought I'd gone too far.

"I've had enough. I got you your answers. The rest is up to Trey."

Duffy sat back down and Matt nuzzled back into her side before I turned to leave. In the kitchen I was about to pass by Marcel, who sat reading at the table. But when he heard me, he looked up from his book and said, "He's not used to seeing her at night. It's upsetting to get the boy out of the routine. You understand this, yes?"

Marcel's accent was French or European Spanish, and in his tone I sensed worry for me or for my opinion of Matt.

"Yeah, I can see how that would upset him." I said this at the back door, just as I opened it to leave.

"During the day, is not the same. Sometimes even when he wake up at night is not the same."

"What do you mean by 'not the same,' Marcel?"

"He's calmer. He could be a regular guy." Marcel struggled to find the right word, so I helped him out.

"You mean *normal?*"

He looked sad and accepted my word with a nod.

"You've known Matt for long?" I asked. What I really wanted to know was, did he know about Matt's violent tendencies, about his having killed Trish, or had it been kept secret from him too?

"Eight years. He is like my own son."

We both turned our heads when Duffy called out loudly from the other room, "I'll get him to bed, Marcel. You can go."

I took one last look at the cozy kitchen, nodded my good-bye to Marcel, and left him at the table with his book.

Once outside, I retraced my steps through the gravel path into the dark gardens and to the front of the estate where I'd left my car. This time I didn't get lost or feel rushed. Suddenly, getting back to my apartment in a hurry wasn't so important.

As I went over the meeting with Matt, I couldn't get past how much he resembled Trey. Even Matt's Afro was kept at the same length as his brother's. I wondered if Matt emulated or looked up to Trey in some perverse way. It was clear by his comment regarding how Trish only fucked Trey that, at the very least, Matt had been jealous of their love. His motive was jealously and unrequited love, as expressed by a schizophrenically skewed and sick mind. Trey and Matt may have been physically identical, but emotionally Matt was no more than a deranged child.

Trey must have known about Matt having killed their sister. How could he not know? If he did, why would he keep the secret? Why wouldn't Trey have reported his brother to the police? The more I tried making sense of the Murphy family, the more fucked up they seemed.

Back at the circular drive, I got into my car and started up the engine, but I didn't move. I looked up at the dark façade of the eerie Tudor building, wondering if I'd ever see it again. It was a sad thought as much as a triumphant one. Maybe my time here was done. Maybe there was no reason for me to ever come back. As gorgeous as the place was, it held a lot of dark secrets and housed people I couldn't fully understand or trust.

The drive home from Pasadena was uneventful and, best of all, pain free. Now that the Vicodin was in full effect, not only had the pain gone but a nice numb daze took over, making everything feel dreamlike.

With the sense of urgency to get home now gone, I looked at the dashboard clock and was surprised to see it was only 11:14. It was relatively early for a weekend night, and the freeways were still crowded with other drivers headed toward late-night destinations. Even if more cars on the freeway meant a slower drive, I wasn't too concerned. Besides, there was a lot for me to mull over.

Matt's role in Trish's death made sense, but coming to terms with my own behavior wasn't so easy. For all this time, I'd suspected and believed Trey to be no less than a monster. Hell, I'd been ready to fucking mutilate my best friend just minutes before, and now everything had changed. *Everything.*

Shouldn't I have been feeling happier knowing my friend wasn't a killer? Now that I knew about Matt's role in the murder, one would think I'd feel relief, like a weight had been lifted. But all I had was a festering sense of guilt and a deep remorse for Trey. I'd really fucked up and caused the guy I'd called my friend unnecessary pain, and probably ruined his opening.

But I'd become so accustomed to hating Trey, so accustomed to believing he'd killed Trish, that part of me found it hard to snap out of the automatic response. What I felt wasn't hatred anymore but confusion.

It was about time I told Trey everything I knew. It was about time I told him about the visions and how accurate they'd been. It was about time I told him all of it. The questions that still lingered would have to wait. I owed Trey that much.

It wasn't until I got to my apartment that the reality of what I'd been about to do really struck me. Once in the bathroom, I froze and looked at the tub, as if seeing it for the first time. It seemed so innocuous a thing—water in a bathtub—but my intentions had been anything but harmless.

After pulling the plug and watching the water swirl down the drain, I envied how easily it washed down to disappear forever, leaving no trace of my intentions behind. But the glare of the ice pick sitting on the edge of the tub wasn't so easy to avoid. With it came a reminder of the misguided rage I'd been carrying. Rage so strong it had made me into a fucking monster. Who was I to be so smug as to judge my friend and decide what his punishment should be? It scared me to consider how far I'd drifted from the guy I thought I was. What had happened to me?

Back in the living room, I twisted open the vodka with no trouble or pain from my hand. I'd set the bottle of pills Duffy had given me on the coffee table, at the ready for when the first pang of pain snuck back. Drinking the smooth clear vodka began to soothe my nerves. I was pouring my second glass when I heard Trey's footsteps climbing the stairs outside.

Odd how, just hours before, all I wanted was to hurt him. And now I wasn't sure how to apologize or redeem myself.

I opened the door and let him in, just like I'd done so many times before. But when he came in, he didn't head for the couch like he usually did. This time Trey stood in the center of the room, his big hoodie draped over his shirt, as he looked around uncomfortably. Or, most likely, insanely pissed. How could I blame him?

"Hey," I offered weakly, sensing not only his disappointment but his tension.

He didn't respond. He slowly walked to the coffee table and stared at the ice pick, the duct tape, and Trish's painting, which sat on the floor and leaned against the television. I'd purposely set them out for him to see, hoping these reminders would help me explain.

But words eluded me. All I could do was watch Trey standing there as he took in the incriminating objects, like a collection that told its own story.

Everything I'd thought about Trey, all the things I'd believed him capable of, flooded through my mind. What the fuck had I been thinking all this time?

As I stood next to him, I began to feel uncomfortable too. He was so still, so silent. I thought he might take a swing at me, maybe pop me one, but he didn't. Sure the Vicodin would keep me pain free for a while, but another hit to the face wasn't something I wanted, even though I probably deserved it.

The least I could do was break the silence. I couldn't just stand there like a pussy and wait for him to talk, so I gave it a try. "Trey, I, um…I haven't been myself, I, ah…Listen, I need to apologize…I was having these weird visions…"

Trey turned to look at me, but there was no surprise in his expression. He avoided the remark about my visions, so I went on.

"I saw you in them…they felt and looked so fucking real, and it wasn't just one vision, there were several. I even saw Rache, before or maybe after she'd gotten into her accident. I also saw Trish—"

Trey interrupted. "And you saw me—or who you thought was me—in these visions, hurting my sister?"

I stopped short, not ready for him to actually know what I meant. "Well, yeah, how did you know?"

"I've had them."

Hearing him say this was an enormous relief, but I stayed cautious, watching him, waiting for him to get mad or scared, but he didn't. He just stood there staring.

Suddenly the stress of the night caught up with me with a swell of fatigue and dizziness. I felt myself sway as I stood, so I sat on the edge of the couch to avoid falling. Mixing Vicodin and vodka wasn't the smartest thing I'd done, and now I struggled to keep my eyes open.

"I loved her," he said, and I believed him now. But there was something missing in his affect. He wasn't talking much, he was keeping quiet.

Either way, it felt weird being with him—so weird, there were moments I wondered if it was another vision. Maybe it was the exhaustion mixed with the drugs and alcohol, because I couldn't remember ever being that tired, that sleepy.

"Listen, I've got to get this out, okay?" I just wanted to confess everything, hoping that if I came clean, he'd forgive me. "In these visions, I saw you hurting her... Trish. You...you bored holes through her mouth so you could—"

"Shut the fuck up!" Trey yelled.

He turned to look down at me, and then he smiled. No smile has ever unnerved me more, it was such a weird-ass smile. He was pissed—and hell, he had every right to be—but why this fucked-up smile? All I could do was nod; doing anything else might set him off again.

"So...you were going to do what exactly...sew me?" He paused and chuckled in disbelief, nodding toward the items on the table. Just then the phone rang, but all I could do was stare at Trey, who talked over the piercing ring. "Pick holes through my face?"

It was my house phone. Since it was a listed number, many of the calls were bogus sales calls, so I'd hooked it up to an old-school answering machine to screen them. The machine picked up after the fourth ring, and since the volume was on mute, it was impossible to hear the message. It didn't matter, I knew who it was. I'd been getting a lot of late-night wrong numbers lately, all from one particular foreign-speaking woman.

These were the thoughts that flashed through my mind while I waited for the fourth ring to sound, just before Trey lunged at me. He came at me as I sat on the edge of the couch, grabbed me by the collar, and pulled me off. I could've fought back, I could've resisted, but I didn't, because more than ever I wanted him to take a swipe at me. In all honesty, I would've been happy to stand there and let him slug away at me. But he didn't. He let me go and turned to leave.

When he got to the door, he said, "I think you should come with me."

"Now?" I asked. "Where?"

He turned and all I could see in his expression was hatred. He was really letting me have it. He was laying on the hate and making me work for forgiveness. Actually, at this point I figured I owed it to him to do whatever he wanted. We'd go for a drive, talk, and we'd work things out. We'd always worked things out in the past, so maybe we would again.

Then he asked, "You think you know so much, don't you?"

Fuck, I didn't know how to answer that. Standing there feeling like a dickhead, I kept quiet. Part of it was the Vicodin, another part was the vodka, but the rest was me not knowing how to make things right between us.

Trey didn't wait for my pathetic answer, he just walked out, leaving the door open behind him. I stood confused, wanting only to go to bed, when the phone started its annoying ringing again. I walked over, picked up the receiver, and let the poor lady have it.

"You got the wrong number, okay? Comprende?" I hung up and left to follow Trey.

As soon as I climbed into his beat-up Toyota, an overwhelming awkwardness swept through me. It occurred to me that things might never be the same in our friendship, and it struck me hard as I sat next to him.

Trey drove without acknowledging me and got on the 10 heading west. He seemed to know where he was going. But where was there to go this late at night? Asking him, or making any type of conversation, seemed too awkward. I got the sense that Trey was working stuff out too, and so I let him drive.

Maybe I should trust him for once. Hell, he could have hit me back at the apartment but didn't. Besides, his deliberate driving convinced me he knew where he was going. There was no aimelssness in his driving, no hesitating at turns or slowing down to read street signs; he just forged ahead in a determined daze. So I didn't ask.

When he got on the highway and sped up, I waited for him to say something to explain where we were headed and why, but he didn't. Without anything to keep me awake, I slid down in my seat, closed my eyes, and although I tried not to, I fell asleep.

Much later, when I pieced that fateful evening together, I would know what had been taking place while I slept in Trey's car. Later I would know that the phone kept ringing back at my apartment. That the caller also tried my cell, which I'd switched off, leaving messages and texts, all of which I would miss until later.

What I'd eventually discover was that the caller was Duffy. When I played the messages later, I would hear a hysteric Duffy sobbing incoherently and with great urgency.

"Matt hurt Trey…Aaron took him to the hospital. Matt…has Trey's car and is headed to your place, don't let him in…YOU HEAR ME? He's…dangerous…Do NOT call the police!" At that point she paused and sobbed some more and then hung up.

So, while I thought I was with Trey, I was really with a somewhat lucid Matt. But of course, I did not know that *yet*.

The car shifted to a sudden, awkward stop, and I woke up with a start. For a split second, I had no idea where I was or how long I'd been asleep. All I knew was that my face was beginning to ache and the old familiar throb was returning.

"Come on, we're here," Trey said, before opening his door to get out. Still exhausted and groggy from my nap, and still under the impression I was with Trey, I lazily watched as he got out and stood by the car to stretch. It took all my will to slide up in my seat, open the door, and join him.

It was dark out, but I could tell we were on a hillside, and even in the darkness I could smell the salt in the cool air and make out the stretch of sand lining the Pacific Ocean just over the cliff side.

"Where are we?" I asked as I took in the surroundings. Behind us was a huge, black, glass and steel structure looming up on the hill. Something about the building looked secret and scientific, like some private medical building or laboratory.

"Come on, we're here to see a friend." He turned and began to walk up the small incline that led to a huge, flat, and mostly empty parking lot.

"Trey, isn't it a little late to be visiting people?" *A friend?* My curiosity was definitely piqued.

"It's fine. It's a hospital. They're open all the time."

So I followed him across the black asphalt and up a grassy hill toward the black glass building. I had no idea what he was up to, but by now Trey had calmed down and seemed to have a purpose. Had I been paying attention, I would have seen the long scar running up his forearm and noticed how, unlike Trey usually did, the guy I was with didn't make eye contact.

There are times when prescient nudges tug and call for your attention—like signs telling you things are out of whack. For some reason I didn't listen or pay attention to those signs, but later, when I looked back and saw things clearly, it was hard to believe I could've been so blind.

TENTH STITCH

We walked up to the front doors of the strange, black, glass and steel hospital. I didn't expect the doors to swoosh open automatically and let us in so easily, but they did. We entered through a cavernous lobby, with a fountain at the center and various seating areas arranged nearby. As much as I looked, there were no signs identifying the name of the place, but, again, this wouldn't occur to me until later.

A bored security guard sitting behind a marble counter raised his head and gave us a heavy-lidded nod as we walked right past him. Needless to say, it appeared security wasn't a major concern in the place.

"Why don't you just tell me what's going on?" I whispered, but Trey, perhaps too caught up in his thoughts, pretended not to hear me. I was about to ask again, when we turned a corner and entered a very different part of the hospital.

This section was different in every way. It even smelled nice. It was high end, swanky, and luxurious. It was more resort hotel than any hospital I'd ever been to. The hallways were wide, and the chandeliers were crystal and set on dimmers to light the space elegantly. The carpets felt thick under my shoes and muffled our steps. Odder still for a hospital were the doors leading into the rooms. They were mahogany, double, and appeared very expensive. *Was it some sort of private hospital?*

Trey's lips moved as he slowed to read the numbers on the brass plates that hung next to every door. He stopped at 188. Unlike the others, these doors were ajar allowing me a brief view of an entry hall inside. My view was cut short because, without stopping to ask me to wait or join him, Trey walked in and closed the doors behind him. Following that, I heard the distinct sound of the deadbolt clicking into place.

As weird as it sounds, I didn't give his behavior much thought. Mostly I wondered where I could sit, since there were no chairs nearby. Finally the exhaustion set in, and I decided to lean against the wall, pull out my cell, and read the first of several texts. My phone had been off all night, so once I switched it on and saw that all the calls and texts were coming from strange numbers, I knew something was up.

Because I didn't have Duffy's number or name programmed into my cell, I had no idea who'd been trying to reach me. Without a name or a recognizable number, it took me a bit of reading to realize they were all from Duffy. Like I always did, I read the last in the thread first, which in this case was a good thing, because it said, "You are not with Trey...You're with Matt. Don't let him take you to Trey's hospital!"

My whole body froze except for my heart. It slapped against my chest like it was trying to jump out. Oh fuck, fuck, fuck. I'd been with Matt this whole time. How could I not know? But why was Trey here, in this hospital?

Although riddled with unanswered questions, there was one thing I was sure of—Matt was dangerous, and I needed to get to him.

"Trey!" I shook the doorknob even though I knew Matt had locked it. "Trey, you in there?"

I kicked at the face of the right door with my boot and pounded it with my palm, hoping Trey would be well enough to get up and let me in.

"Trey! Just get to the door!" I was calling out as loudly as I could, pounding harder against the thick doors. "Trey!"

I stood back and kicked at the center, where the doors came together, knowing it was the weakest point. "Matt, I know it's you. Open the door!"

I was running out of time, Trey might be too hurt or drugged to defend himself. Matt could kill him if I took too long. With more determination, I stood back and away from the doors, raised my leg, and kicked hard, this time using the sole of my boot until the doors gave a little in the center. I kicked again and again until the right door flew open.

I walked inside slowly, expecting Matt to jump out at me from some corner, but instead I saw him curled up against a wall, his face hidden in his hands and his shoulders shaking.

"Where the fuck is Trey?" I yelled as I approached him, smelling the urine before I noticed the darkness at the crotch of his jeans where he'd wet himself. He made a pitiful figure—a crying, man-sized child who'd pissed his pants, curled up on the floor. Had I not known how capable of cruelty he was, I might've felt sorry for him.

"Answer me, where is Trey?"

Matt huddled into himself and sobbed some more, but didn't speak.

I looked around the room, saw the Le Corbusier couch, among other the high-end pieces, stylishly mixed in with antiques, and knew this wasn't a regular room. I wasn't in a regular hospital. It was too spacious, too personal, and too fucking luxurious to be anything but residential and private.

"Matt, where are we?"

I kicked his leg to get some reaction from him, but all he did was look up at me with a tear-streaked, contorted face to say, "Leave me alone!"

I turned from Matt when I heard a noise, which could have been my imagination or a movement from a nearby room. There was a large picture window overlooking the ocean on one side of the living room, with two empty wingback chairs facing it, so the sound couldn't have come from there.

I left Matt to look inside the adjoining room, a large, unlit bedroom with an empty and unmade bed. When I stepped in, the motion sensor caused the lights to come on, and suddenly the room went from dim to fully lit. At the bed, I flipped the cover to be sure it was empty before heading into the attached bathroom, where the light also came on, revealing a glitzy, marble-and-glass shower in one corner and a Jacuzzi tub in the other. Both were vacant.

By the time I made it back to the living room, I was growing more confused, but my confusion was muffled by my urgency to find Trey. Losing my patience for Matt, I rushed toward where he sat slumped and sniveling on the floor and grabbed him. An impatient rage welled up inside me as I yanked at his shirt front to lift him from the floor, before yelling into his pitiful face, "Where is he?"

Holding him only by his collar, I lifted until I had him at eye level. I waited for him to respond, but all he did was sob, so I slammed him hard against the wall before releasing my grip. Instead of standing, Matt collapsed onto the floor with a thump. He settled back into the same crouched position until I picked him up, this time using one hand to lift and the other to slam his face. The thing was, my fist landed on the bony part of his cheek, and it wasn't until it was way too late to stop that I remembered my injured hand. It took a fraction of a second for the painful hot sensation to shoot a searing shockwave from my knuckles up my arm and into my shoulder.

"Fuck, fuck, fffffaaawwwk!" I yelled as the agony coursed through me. When I looked up, a bloodied Matt stood right in my face. I happily noticed I'd knocked out one of his front teeth. From where I stood so close to him, his smell, his sickness, his pissed pants, his putrid breath, were so strong that my desire to kill him was hard to resist. So, with enormous restraint, I pushed him in disgust and back onto the floor.

Matt raised his head to aim his outburst toward the window. "Trey's a fucker." He was bawling harder now, just like he had when I'd seen him at the cottage. There was no mistaking him for Trey now. In this state, he was just as irrational as a disgruntled toddler.

Somehow he stopped himself from crying, and with a mixture of fear and hatred in his eyes he whispered, "You should've minded your own business and left us alone."

Then he leaned his head back and squealed out as loudly as he could, once again aiming his question toward the window. "Why not me?"

He was definitely talking to someone by the window. Was Trey in one of the chairs, fast asleep, or worse?

As I slowly approached the two chairs, I noticed one hadn't been empty like I'd assumed before. The shadow of this chair included two bottom shadows, which had to be feet. As I focused harder, I made out small black shoes. Shoes and feet too small, too childlike to belong to Trey. With my next steps, I saw the back of a small head and then hair, but it wasn't Trey's short black afro, this hair was straight and brown.

Circling toward the front of the chair, I noticed a woman's scarred hand resting on the armrest and what looked like a mutilated face partially hidden by thin, brown hair. The hand, although heavily scarred, managed to maintain a tight hold on a revolver. The reddish skin looked white and lumpy where the fingers gripped the gun.

I remember thinking the light might've been playing tricks on me, that maybe shadows were to blame for the illusion that the woman's face was mutilated, but the more I looked, the more I realized no shadow could create such a disquieting effect.

The woman raised her face to look at me. Instead of meeting her gaze, I averted my eyes briefly. I had to. Sure, I felt like shit for looking away, but it was too much to register at once. When I did look back at her, she hadn't flinched or moved her face. She kept it raised as if wanting to be sure I got a good look at it.

Outside of the darker hair color, there was little for me to go on to be sure it was her... except for the ten, red, welt-like scars running neatly above and below her lips. Five above her top lip, and five below her lower lip.

It was Trish.

"Not a pretty sight, am I?" It was her voice. Gone from it were the innocence and the wonder so prevalent in her recordings, but it was her voice.

To explain someone's appearance after being mutilated is difficult. I'd never met or seen Trish in person before. I'd only seen her in visions or in old photographs. It was obvious there'd been attempts to recreate her face with plastic surgery. Mostly in places where her facial bones had been smashed when Matt had taken the metal baseball bat to her, but none of it seemed to have helped her look...*normal*.

"I...I thought you were dead...I saw him smashing your...I'm sorry...." It was an outburst I regretted the second it came out. I'd said it without thinking, without considering how it might make her feel.

"There are days when I wish I were," Trish said, this time turning her head to address Matt. When she did, I noticed the missing ear, the one that had been ripped off during the beating. During one of the first visions, the one in the basement, where I'd had trouble making out or identifying the bloody mass Matt had left on the concrete floor, I'd seen the severed ear.

The ear must have been too unsalvageable to be reattached. The result was that her head appeared unnaturally flat on the side where the ear had once been.

The thing that struck me most was how Matt's insanity and capacity for cruelty were more glaring when I took in the result than when I'd watched him in the violent process. I glanced toward Matt, who had gone back to crouching in the corner to resume his weeping.

Bending down toward Trish in the chair, I placed my hand over hers. It was an automatic reaction, and as naturally as it came to me, I sensed it made her uncomfortable. She gripped the gun tightly until I cautiously lifted my hand and took the gun from her without resistance. I set it on her lap before curling my fingers around her smaller and slighter ones.

I held her hand like that—mine over hers—for what seemed like minutes. At one point I loosened my hold to let go, but Trish held on, squeezing my hand in silent encouragement.

"Did you like my paintings?" She looked away into the black Pacific.

"You knew Trey was showing them?"

Trish chuckled before explaining. "I asked him to. I still paint. It's what keeps me alive." Trish paused, then briefly looked at me before gazing back out the window and into the darkness. "Trey called before Matt got to him. Told me he'd sold all but two of the smaller ones and got a commission. He was on his way over. It's why I left the door open."

I turned to make sure Matt was still crouched and against the wall before asking, "Did he hurt you? Matt, I mean?"

Trish shook her head. "All I had to do was show him the gun. It's the only thing he's afraid of."

"Duffy—ah, your mom tried to call me. She said Trey was in the hospital—"

"She called here too. Trey will be fine."

I relaxed at hearing Trey wasn't badly hurt.

The fact that I was talking to Trish was strange. Just seeing her alive was disconcerting. Saying the right thing, or not saying the *wrong* thing, was making me overthink my words. I needed to slow down, relax, and maybe let Trish set the pace.

She seemed strangely calm sitting in her chair. Her attention was seemingly focused on the vague outline of ocean outside, and yet something about her demeanor gave the impression she was taking the time to gather her thoughts.

It suddenly made sense. Trey had been having the show for Trish. It'd been arranged by the two of them as a way to maintain her anonymity. After all, it was about the art, not the artist.

I let go of Trish's hand and stood to drag the other wing chair nearer to hers. Once I sat down, I felt the fatigue kick in and I wondered if I'd ever have enough strength to get up. Before settling, I made sure to check on Matt, who was still on the floor, his mouth slightly agape while he slept. He was clearly conked out.

For what felt like a lifetime, I sat next to Trish and looked out the big window. At first the view outside appeared mainly black, but the darkenss was deceptive. Once I allowed my eyes to adjust, more and more details became apparent. The contrast of the sand on the shore—a lighter grey than the charcoal of the Pacific it lined—began to take shape. The sky beyond it, a shade lighter than the ocean, held streaks of pale clouds. And although the waves were small, each seemed to carry a white mass of foam at its crest, delivering each to the edge of the shore where it disappeared into the sand.

All the variations of grey, all the possible nuances of black mixed with white distinguished one aspect of the scenery from the other, differentiating details and adding depth in the most subtle of ways. The ocean would have been just a solid black mass without the touches of white mixing in to create greys, distinguishing sand from water, water from sky. It reminded me of Trey's claim of how mixing the two shades only resulted in a muting, as if to suggest each shade was degraded in the mixing. If Trey had been there, I would've used the view to illustrate how the mixing of the two shades was what made distinction possible.

After a night of flux and conflict, I began to relax. It felt natural, my being with Trish, and yet there was a finality to it, a feeling that I may only get to do it once. This feeling led me to savor every moment and mark everything I felt, saw, or said, as if for posterity.

When Trish broke the silence, her tone was cautious. "You should get help."

Without her having to explain what she meant, I'd come to accept that there was something wrong with me. Even if the visions had all panned out to be real, I couldn't go on living like that, always on the edge, always wondering if what I saw was real or not.

But there was something more pressing, something I couldn't leave Trish without asking, "Did you see me? When Matt was hurting you, could you see me?" As soon as I asked, I noticed her body shift uncomfortably in the chair.

"I don't remember lots of things...It doesn't really matter now."

But I was sure she'd seen me. I remembered our eyes meeting while she'd been in the tub, the look of recognition had been real and distinct. Then I remembered how she'd clamped her eyes shut as soon as she'd seen me, as if to wipe the vision of me away. Why would she lie? Could it be Trish had learned to quell her own visions? If she had seen me, the only reason not to acknowledge it would be to maintain a hold on reality. The same hold I was losing a grip on.

Now that I sat next to her, with the overhead light casting a harsher glow on her face, a light that sharpened scars and emphasized the lack of bone structure, I could still see the precocious girl Trish had been. With her chin raised, her focused eyes, and her pursed lips, no amount of scar tissue could erase her soul or her essence.

"Trish, please tell me if you remember seeing me." My voice sounded urgent, even to me. This was my chance to talk to someone who knew about the visions, my chance to talk to someone who knew how horrific they were, someone who had been there.

"Matt saw you. He said so when he got here."

Did she think I was crazy like Matt? Did she think I might hurt...? The thought was too much for me to handle. "I'm not like him."

As I said this, the image of what I had been ready to do that night raced through my memory. The tub filled with water, the bags of ice in my freezer, the ice pick, the duct tape, the needle threaded with yarn—it hit me like a hard slap of realization. But instead of a calm or sensible reflection, an inner rage of denial shook me. I was different, I told myself. I'd been ready to act out revenge and nothing else.

Trish continued to look out at the shadowy beauty beyond. She doubted me, and I needed to clear the air. She needed to know I was on her side.

"You think I'm like Matt?" I leaned forward on the chair and noticed how Trish flinched. "Okay, listen, I thought I was losing it, going crazy, until I started to piece together that everything—*everything*—I saw in those visions, Trish, really happened. I wasn't making any of that shit up."

She didn't seem to believe me, so I asked about the most innocuous, the most inoffensive memory I had. "Pink phone cover. You had a pink cell phone cover—Am I right?"

She looked at me strangely and nodded, but her expression could've been one of appeasement as opposed to acceptance. She also seemed unwilling or too cautious to react to the new urgency in my tone. If she was threatened by my anger, my insistence, she didn't show it. Instead she maintained her gaze on the blackness outside the window. Finally, when she spoke, her voice was yielding.

"No, you're not like Matt."

Here she stopped and looked down at her hands nervously before going on. "I saw him talking to someone once, maybe twice, when he was hurting me. Like he saw someone there with us. It was a flash of a memory and I'd all but forgotten it until now." Trish paused and exhaled deeply, before going on. "Earlier, when he first barged in, Matt kept saying you were the guy, the one he'd seen in the bathroom. He said you tried to get in the way."

Trish's eyes were wet with tears, and I felt like shit for bringing this up, for being defensive. I reached out to touch her, but she shook her head in refusal. At first I wondered if she was disgusted by me, but when she went on, I realized this was something else entirely. It was Trish being strong, holding on to her own sanity.

"I tried not to look at or focus on Matt or on anything else. I could feel the babies were gone, and I hated myself for feeling grateful." Trish's eyes were wet, and she raised a hand to wipe the side of her face. "I didn't want them to feel pain. I was afraid my babies could feel what I was feeling, not just the pain, but the terror."

Trish finally turned to me, and although her eyes were filled with tears, she smiled sadly.

"Trish, I did everything in my power to help you. I wanted to get you out."

She smiled again, that same sad smile, and a rush of peace, of well-being overwhelmed me. Even with this newfound comfort, I wasn't ready for what she said next.

"I may not have seen you, but it's reassuring that I wasn't totally alone with Matt. Not being alone in your nightmare helps, if that makes any sense."

She reached over and put her hand on my shoulder, and I wanted to hold it. I wanted to get up and hold all of Trish and comfort her, but I didn't. Something inside stopped me from reaching out.

Taking her hand away, Trish laid her head back on the chair and closed her eyes. After a while she said, "You'll have to take him away."

She meant Matt, who was still out cold on the floor. "Why would Matt bring me here?"

"Who knows? In Matt's fucked-up mind, it could be he wanted you to know I was still alive...or to hurt you. It's hard to say."

Trish stood up and walked to the window. She glanced back, toward the huddled form of her half brother on the floor and then back to me. She wore an oversized sweatshirt and jeans, which made her look small, even smaller than I'd imagined. With her hands stuck inside the pockets of her sweatshirt, she gestured toward where Matt lay.

"I told Duffy I'd give her an hour to come get him. If she's late, I told her I'd shoot him, *then* call the police."

My eyes immediately went down to where she kept her hands in her pockets, where the butt of her small but undoubtedly effective gun stuck out. I had to give it to her; she could have shot Matt and no one would have questioned or blamed her. Not after Matt's history, his brutal assault, and the murder of the twins had been exposed. Part of me wished she had shot Matt, so the cruel Murphy family secrets would be out in the public, where they could see light and maybe justice.

"She's been protecting Matt all these years." I wasn't asking as much as spelling it out for myself. How Duffy had kept him protected and away from the world in that cabin under the loving care of Marcel, how fearful she'd been I'd call the police, all of it suddenly made sense. "She protected him, while you...while you were here."

Trish interrupted suddenly. "I don't need Duffy or want anything to do with her. She has always been a self-serving bitch. It's my dad who pays the bills here. I'll always have him, Trey, and my art."

"It's why Trey doesn't want anything to do with her." I suddenly understood everything. I understood why the last thing Trish needed was to see Matt or Duffy again.

"So, if you don't mind, could you see him out, and wait for Duffy away from here?" Her expression was pleading but forceful.

At least for once, Trish's welfare needed to come first. She'd taken enough shit for a lifetime. So I nodded, turned, and walked over to Matt's slumped form. I grabbed him off the floor and half dragged, half carried him out of Trish's apartment, ignoring his protests all the way. At the doors, I pushed him into the hallway and watched as he stumbled but gathered his balance enough to lean against the wall behind him.

He blinked and cocked his head before smiling up at me. "You are like me." He laughed and slapped his thigh and shook his head, like we were sharing some fucking joke.

Closing the doors on Matt, I walked back in to say good-bye to Trish, when a sudden, heavy feeling of sadness choked me, a sense that I might never see her again. At least I'd have one last word with her, some parting word of kindness, something to let her know I cared.

When I found her, she was slipping off her shoes and sitting on the edge of her bed. She must have sensed me at the door, because she looked up and waited. All the things I wanted to say, all the things I would later wish I'd said, escaped me. I simply stood at her bedroom door and muttered, "Good-bye, Trish."

Her eyes seemed to shine when she held my gaze, smiled, and said, "Good-bye."

EPILOGUE

I WOULD NEVER SEE TRISH AGAIN, but I would ask Trey about her from time to time. Occasionally I'd suggest joining him during one of his frequent visits, but each time I did, he'd explain how Trish didn't want visitors, not even me. It pleased me, however, to discover she asked after me, and sent me her best.

My new business slugged along, and Tina continued to bring me work, until my breakdown. While still lucid enough, I called to thank her for her support, but told her I would be going away. When she asked where, I was blunt and honest, admitting that I didn't really know. After an awkward silence, she wished me luck and suggested I get back to her when I was up and running my business again.

It was the truth too. I didn't know where I was going. What I did know I couldn't tell her or anyone else, not even Trey. What I did know was that living in my apartment was no longer comfortable for me. It didn't feel like a home anymore; it had become a foreign space where my sanity was at constant risk. Because most of my visions had occurred in my apartment, I came to think of being alone and holed up in a private space as a risky endeavor. Sure, I'd had visions when I was out, but those were less frightening and much more containable.

Being in public during a vision used to be frightening. Now it felt like the very best place for me to be. In public, I had the security of being among the masses, and the certain reality of everyday people doing everyday things to keep me in check. At least I thought so at the time.

Before letting the apartment go, I went about ridding myself of things I didn't want or need. What was meant as a purging of excess material possessions became a Zen-like act of personal cleansing. I sold most of my furniture, and what didn't sell, Stan, my neighbor, was happy to take. Since he was moving into my place, switching it out for his downstairs apartment, leaving him the heavier things was a relief. He kept my drafting table (said he'd use it as a bar), my bed, and offered me a hundred bucks for my computer.

Of the things I kept, all either held emotional significance or were necessary for survival. I kept my dad's old longboard and the vinyl record albums he'd given me, but I sold the record player. Everything I didn't want or need went out the door without one ounce of regret. Of all my clothes, I kept only what would fit in the trunk of my car.

Once everything was gone, a peculiar irony occurred to me: without all those things, I no longer really needed an apartment. To think, all those things I housed were why I needed physical space in the first place. Why people did this—chose to live this way—became less logical and more of a mystery to me. In my new way of thinking, the fewer things one had, the less encumbered your life was. But then, I'd succumbed to the very same compulsion to secure a space of my own. Once I had, it seemed the hoarding followed naturally. Funny how the less I had, the freer I felt.

Trey and I made up, but our relationship changed. He looked at me differently now, but only when he didn't think I noticed. He didn't understand my uncut and unwashed hair or the beard that was growing in, or my need to feel unfettered by physical things. But how could he? He was rolling in sales and demand for his work. He still showed Trish's work, but he also showed his own, including a pretty badass portrait he did of me standing behind Flaco's shop, where I kept my car, with my dad's gunner tied to the roof and packed with all my stuff.

The portrait Trey painted of me sold to a large and powerful Los Angeles art collector, which caused Trey's art credibility to skyrocket. As the subject of his piece, I became the focus of hipsters, who suddenly wanted to interview me for local papers or come by Flaco's to "talk" and meet the guy in the painting—me. I knew they thought me interesting and were honestly intrigued by my leaving everything to live out of my car, but there was also something else. I got the sense they were too careful, too cautious around me, as if they thought I'd lose my cool if they said something offensive or asked something too personal or whatever.

The portrait itself was, like I said, badass and made me look like some modern-day renegade. In it, I'm leaning against the side of my car out behind Martha's Mom, where Flaco keeps crates, trash dumpsters and pallets, and where two huge oak trees offer shade. My arms are crossed over my chest, making me seem totally relaxed, and I'm facing directly out, so if you looked at the painting I'd be looking right at you with my full-on beard and dirty jeans.

One journalist from a Westside paper wrote, "Meeting this guy who lives out of his car, who only drives it to go surfing, is like coming face to face with a modern-day version of Manet's *The Ragpicker*." Funny thing was, I remember seeing that painting tons of times with my grandfather as a kid. He'd taken me to the Norton Simon Museum, in Pasadena, countless times as a way to introduce me to great art. *The Ragpicker* had been one of my favorite paintings. It seems that painting, the one I'd loved as a kid, somehow resonated with me in a silent, deeply prophetic way.

Flaco came through as a new friend. He said the guy who'd held him up the night of Trey's opening, the guy I'd seen pointing the gun at him, would have shot him for sure if the cops hadn't shown up. He said my making Saffron, the chick in the coffee shop, call the police was what saved his life. For that, Flaco said he'd be happy to have me live in and guard the backyard of his store. Good guy Flaco often left sandwiches, extra blankets, and food out for me too.

Being on my own feels real and right. Being on my own means total freedom. Had I not had the freedom, I wouldn't have had time to write this story. Sharing the events of those few months and going over those memories so carefully wouldn't have been possible. My ability to document the visions, to mark each and every important detail of what I saw, of what I learned, became possible only after my liberation from conventional living.

There are times, when it's dark and late and I'm having trouble sleeping, when I'll remember how Trish had cautioned me the night I met her. I'll remember her quietly uttering, "You should get help." When she'd said it, I remember having a fleeting thought of a kindly doctor or psychiatrist who would guide me through reconciling my visions, like balancing a checkbook. Someone who might be able to check off each vision and match it up to every reality it corresponded to. Maybe the hypothetical therapist could've explained how a guy like me can be called crazy, when all his visions and hallucinations had been real. How could I be labeled a schizophrenic— which is what I'd heard Flaco once say to a customer who'd called me "a creepy dude," if all my visions were real? If so, it wasn't my brain that was marred, it was something else. The only downside was, I couldn't name what that something else was.

Even so, over time, the sense of my needing help vanished, and my getting therapy or meds became less important the more time I spent living on the streets.

The truth is, the more I get to know myself, the more comfortable I get being in my own skin, and the more I'm convinced people are wrong about me being crazy. No drug or talk therapy, no amount of time spent in a treatment facility could offer me the independence, happiness, and freedom I've found on my own on the streets. Maybe one day I'll change my mind, but for now this is exactly how I want to live: more invisible than the invisible man.

Should you ever walk on Melrose Avenue in LA and notice a tall, skinny blond guy with a red beard, you might try calling out a hello—but then, you wouldn't know my name, would you?

28837063R00065

Made in the USA
Lexington, KY
03 January 2014